THE CANDY CANE KILLER

A chilling crime thriller with a stunning final twist

EMMY ELLIS

DI Bethany Smith Book 6

Originally published as *The Gift is Murder*

JOFFE BOOKS

Revised edition 2023
Joffe Books, London
www.joffebooks.com

First published in Great Britain in 2019
as *The Gift is Murder*

This paperback edition was first published
in Great Britain in 2023

Cover art by Dee Dee Book Covers

ISBN: 978-1-83526-161-3

PROLOGUE

Christmas. It brought back memories.
Terrible, terrible memories.

In the darkness of the Christmas-week night, she stared down at the lowlife sitting on the kerb. Filthy bastard. Unkempt, he was, probably on drugs or riddled with alcohol. One of the dregs of society. A forgotten. A man down on his luck, a brown-haired scuzz-bucket who needed a week-long soak in the bath before he'd look anywhere near presentable.

She shuddered.

"How are you tonight, my child?" She bent over, her black robe swishing around her legs. "Do you need sustenance?" Such a good word, that. It fitted with who she seemed. A caring person. Someone who used those kinds of words.

The vagrant stared up at her, blue eyes empty, then they filled with hope: *Will you feed me? Help me find a place to stay?*

Yes, she'd do that, only not in the way he might think.

"Food," she explained, in case he was a bit slow on the uptake, one of those useless prats who hadn't made use of the free education system. "Do you need something to eat?" She laughed inwardly at her affected tone, the way she sounded gentle. He'd better fall for her guise, otherwise, all this would have been for nothing.

He nodded, this twenty-something, in dirty clothes that appeared to have come from an eighties jumble sale. Maybe he'd visited the shelter at some point and they'd kitted him out in the ridiculous gear. He'd have a story as to how he'd become homeless, no doubt, one he rattled on about to anyone who'd listen, and she supposed *she'd* have to hear him out in order for him to trust her.

She sat on the frosty pavement beside him, the cold seeping through her habit, and got a whiff of beggar's stench for her trouble, the kind of aftershave they all carried on themselves. Unwashed skin, body odour and that musty, mouldy scent.

"So," she said. "Tell me your story." A smile had worked wonders when she'd practised on previous evenings, so she gave him one, teeth on show, the lot, the winter air nipping at her balled cheeks.

He stared at her, frowning, but it melted away, much like she wished the smattering of snow would. His forehead smoothed out, and he smiled back.

"You're kidding me," he said. "You *want* to know my story?"

"Of course. All God's children deserve to be heard." She didn't hold with any of that old guff, but it was what would be expected of her. She didn't even believe the love of a deity existed. "Let it all out. It'll be cathartic."

And then he was off, lamenting about how his mother had kicked him out for nicking a phone off some kid at school. How he'd needed it so he could sell the thing and make a bit of cash to pay the bullies. Fifteen, he'd been, desperate to be liked, but those bullies, they'd taunted him and pushed him to steal.

A likely excuse. This twat could have said no, stood up for himself and kicked them in the knackers. Instead, he'd *chosen* to obey them, and look where it had got him.

You did the same thing once. Obeyed.

She shoved that thought away. No sense in dredging up her own past. She was a different person now. Older. Wiser.

And if she had to do it all over again, she'd tell her bully to shove her meanness up her skinny arse. She'd tell her abuser to shove his dick in someone else. She'd *leave*, not wait to be thrust out into the unknown. She'd call the shots, not the other way around.

"What's your name?" she asked.

"Karl. What's yours?"

"Sister Leeanne."

"Right."

"Would you like to come back with me? You can have a shower, some food. A bed for the night. I hate to think of you out here alone. You're so young. It's tragic that you've spent ten years wandering the streets. Twenty-five is no age to be destitute."

That came out all right, didn't it? She could almost be mistaken for someone who gave a massive toss.

"Is that allowed?" He frowned again. "I mean, won't the other nuns wonder what you're doing with someone like me?"

"No. Besides, they'll all be in bed."

"Okay then."

He got up stiffly, as if his bones were as old as dirt, while she sprang up, nimble from the karate she'd taught herself off YouTube. She led him along, snow dancing in the halo glow from lampposts, drifting down to settle on the ground. She shoved her hands into her sleeves, appearing more like a sister of God by the second, while he shuffled, lagging, annoying her because he wasn't shifting his arse into gear. You'd think the promise of grub and a bed would urge him on, but no, he took his time.

Well, she'd be having some fun with him soon, and he'd wish he'd never been so greedy. It always got you in the end, the need for more. He'd be praying to be back on the streets before long.

Shame he'd never get there.

This man didn't deserve to live after what he'd put her through.

CHAPTER ONE

Karl Hartley. His full name seemed foreign to him now, belonging in another life, to another person. He didn't really need his surname these days anyway. People didn't tend to ask unless it was for signing in at the shelter, so for the rest of the time, it was just Karl.

Sister Leeanne stood over by the sink in the nunnery, filling a saucepan with water to soak it, the one she'd cooked his beans in. That was what he'd asked for, beans on toast, a reminder of his childhood when it had actually been okay. A happy place, not like now. Mind you, he was happy for the moment and had come up trumps by being brought here. Who would have thought changing his usual nighttime location would have led to this? A hot meal in an old-fashioned kitchen, in a church-like house, drinking a nice cup of tea from a china mug instead of one of those beige plastic ones the shelter handed out.

She'd appeared from nowhere, an angel sent to save him, even if only for tonight. He'd enjoy the experience while he could. No point worrying about tomorrow, when he'd be turfed out into the snow, same as the night Mum had done it.

He shivered, despite the warmth. Flames flickered and raged in the grate behind him, and he supposed all ancient houses had fireplaces, although he'd spotted a radiator in the hallway — or 'foyer' as she'd called it. A wooden pew was out there, too, standing against the wall on the dark-grey slate tiles, and it made sense, what with her being holy and all that. The place was massive, big enough for ten nuns to sleep under the black-beamed ceilings, tucked up nice and cosy.

"I bet it's lovely to be clean again," she said, placing the pan on the draining board and coming to sit at the table with him.

He nodded. It *was* lovely. He'd all but forgotten what it was like until he'd stepped under the hot spray and all the odours of being homeless disappeared beneath the Palmolive lather. She had dead posh shampoo an' all, the kind that cost the same as a coffee from Starbucks, all thick bubbles when he'd massaged it into his scalp. Funny that she had men's deodorant on the bathroom windowsill, though. Maybe she'd bought it for people like him. Tramps she'd saved before.

"It's like I'm normal again," he said, still hungry, even though he'd eaten all his food, like now he knew there was more available, his stomach griped for it. Still, he'd better not fill up too much. She'd warned him he might be sick if he did. Bellies that had been empty for too long didn't take kindly to a feast, she'd said. Besides, she had more food he could have later.

"Do you want another tea?" She rose, all ethereal, a floating apparition, and moved to the silver kettle.

"Yes, please." This was surreal. Couldn't be happening. Had he fallen backwards on the pavement from sheer exhaustion and was dreaming? Good shit like this didn't happen to him.

While she busied herself, he stared out of the window. The sky had a weird glow, as if the snowflakes had lit it up, and the white stuff fell steadier now, thicker, with the intent to settle, he reckoned. He'd have to risk sleeping in the old warehouse over the coming nights, hoping the others wouldn't steal his boots while he was sparko. They did that, every man or woman for themselves, but he wasn't giving them up. He'd pinched them from the back of Sports Direct when a delivery bloke had gone inside the shop and left the pallet out in the open.

"There," she said. "Get that down you."

Startled out of his thoughts, he jumped a bit then took the fresh cup out of her smooth hands. The sight of them brought home how chapped his were. She picked up the dirty mug and returned to the sink, keeping her back to him.

"Thanks again," he said.

"No, thank *you*."

He frowned. "What for?"

"Well, you trusted me. Came here."

That thing on her head was like black material hair falling down her back. It had a white band at the front, across her forehead and over her ears, and he wondered what her real hair was like. Blonde, he imagined, going by her light-brown eyebrows.

He'd swear her shoulders were shaking. Was she crying?

"Are you all right?" he asked, anxious.

"Yes," she said, the word strangled.

He eased to the side so he could check out her reflection in the window. She was smiling, her mouth open, same as when you laughed, so that put him at ease. He didn't like crying women. They scared him. Mum had always gone off on one when the tears came, lashing out at him, a punch to the gut, a kick in the ribs. Although life had been hard since she'd told him to leave, he was glad she had. Living with her had become a nightmare once she'd lost her job and turned to Gordon's Gin for company. Gordon told her to be nasty, to blame Karl for everything. Shame the copious amounts of Nescafé the next day hadn't told her to say sorry.

"Yes, you enjoy that," Sister Leeanne said. "Then you can go to the room I've rigged up for you."

'Rigged up' was a bit of a weird expression, but he wouldn't waste any time thinking about it. He blew on his tea, then sipped. It seemed different to the other one, a tad bitter if he were honest, but that might be because he had the taste of beans on his tongue. Regardless, he'd drink it, thankful for two cups in one sitting. That was unheard of these days. As Curmudgeon was fond of saying, someone up there was looking after Karl today. The old boy had been a tramp for longer than Karl, and they met up from time to time on their travels, plus whenever he stayed at the warehouse. Not that Karl travelled anywhere much except for walking around Shadwell. He knew every nook and cranny. That was what ten years of traipsing it did for you, and he'd told himself when he'd caught a bus here all that time ago that this would be the place he'd see out his days.

Half of his tea had gone, but he couldn't remember drinking it. He shrugged, eyes getting heavy, and finished it off. Sister Leeanne would show him to his room soon, she'd said so earlier, and he couldn't wait to snuggle up under a duvet, a squishy pillow beneath his head. A mattress was his idea of heaven.

"Ooh, you look like you're about to drop off," she said, coming over to stand by his side.

Woozy wasn't the word. Had she put a nip of brandy in the tea or what? Was that why it'd tasted funny? He stared up at her. Two faces, fuzzy, and she zoomed down at him, her nose touching his.

"Almost there," she said and drew back a bit, her eyes wide, her lips pulled back to reveal her teeth.

But it didn't seem like a smile this time, more of a snarl.

"This is going to be suicide." She straightened.

What was she on about?

Blackness crowded his peripheral, reaching out to merge with her dress and headgear, and she was just a floating face, bobbing around, laughter burbling from a mouth the shape of an orange segment. His eyes snapped shut, and he couldn't open them for the life of him. He was pulled into sleep, his body seeming to sink into the chair, and the last thing he recalled was his head tipping to the side, his cheek wanting to be best friends with his shoulder.

* * *

Sister Leeanne's voice penetrated his brain, but try as he might, Karl couldn't open his eyes. His whole body was heavy, and his neck hurt, bent as it was, his chin resting on his chest. His position didn't make sense. It was as though he dangled, except something was between his legs, holding him up. A pole?

"Stirring, are we, dickhead?"

Sister Leeanne didn't sound the same. It was her, definitely, but her voice was so much harsher than he remembered. And . . . dickhead?

He tried to part his lips, to say something, but they wouldn't move. He became more alert, albeit imprisoned inside a body that wouldn't work. His brain was lucid now, and warning bells went off. Why, though? She was a nun, had helped him, fed him. There was no way a woman like her would do anything to him, so how come he was worried?

"You're him, the one," she said. "But I'm warning you, if you don't do what I want, I won't be pleased."

A slap to his face had his head snapping to the side, and at last, he managed to open his eyes.

What. The. Fuck?

There was no way he was seeing this. A wall. Rough, light-pink plaster. Drawings on it done with what might be charcoal and red paint. People with facial deformities, their jagged, pointy teeth bared. Hands, hairs on the backs, long claws at the ends of spindly fingers, holding a blood-drenched heart. A torso, sliced down the middle, intestines spilling out, lumpy snakes. Men with no dicks. So many, many images he couldn't bear to look at.

He turned his head, peering around for her, but she wasn't there. The room . . . Oh God, it was empty except for him. Karl stared down at himself. Naked. A length of metal sticking out from under his balls. A strap around his middle holding him to something. He couldn't part his legs or manoeuvre to see what it was, so he reached behind, his palm coming into contact with something furry. He shouted out in fear, snatching his hand away, and Sister Leeanne jumped out to land in front, her long blonde hair mussed on top.

He'd touched her head.

What the hell had she been doing crouching back there?

She wasn't the nun he knew, but someone else, her lips black, eyeshadow the same, even beneath her lower lashes, giving the impression she had severe bags. That *Beetlejuice* character, minus the manky teeth. She splayed her fingers beside her, the bones in her hands standing out in sharp relief. Her white nightgown covered her from neck to slippered feet, something an old dear would wear, not a young woman like her. She tilted her head, first one way, then the other, and shivers scattered up his spine.

"I am not Felicity Gray tonight," she said.

What?

"It's morning. Everywhere is white. So white." She pressed her pointer fingers to her temples and wiggled her hands. Glared, her cheeks so pale it had to be makeup. "No, this is right, Stout Farmer. It's *right.*" She blinked. Peered at Karl. "Oh. No windows for you to see out of, sausage man."

What the bloody hell is she talking about? Who is Stout Farmer? Sausage man?

She smiled. "Time for breakfast."

She disappeared behind him, and fear climbed into his gut, settling down for the duration. His bladder protested, and he pissed, ashamed of the sound of it slapping onto the slate tiles, and he wished he was back on the streets, hungry and alone.

"You dirty fucker," she said, appearing again, pushing a hostess trolley. It had a silver dome on top, a fork next to it, plus a plastic cup with a red straw leaning on the inside. She lifted the dome and put it on her head. "Nice helmet, eh?"

What is wrong with this woman?

He gaped at her, hoping this was a nightmare, his hands shaking so much they slapped at his outer thighs. She picked up the fork, and he gawped at what was on the plate. Red, so much red. Flesh, raw, and that tripe shit his nan used to buy.

"Yum, yum, pig's bum." She laughed, an alarming trill, and jabbed the fork at the pile of crimson mess. "Open wide, the aeroplane is coming!"

She zoomed the laden fork towards him, and it bumped into his closed lips.

"You *will* eat this," she snapped. "No, Baker Mother, he can't have a muffin instead."

He wanted to cry. What she was saying made no sense. He tried to kick out, to lift his arms and punch her face, but his body wouldn't comply, his stupid hands still slapping his legs. She stabbed the fork into the flesh on the plate, and it stood up by itself. She vanished behind him again, coming back with some kind of device. Pressing it to his cheek, she pushed a button, and his mouth snapped open, pain searing into him, an electric shock. Then she rammed a plastic, rectangular frame between his teeth. He automatically bit down, tears of agony streaming. She placed the device on the trolley, then shovelled food onto his tongue. If he had his way, he'd spit it out, but he couldn't.

"Swallow it," she ordered and tipped his head back, banging it on whatever he was strapped to.

He choked, trying desperately to do as she'd asked, the taste of blood heavy, the nectar of Hell. The mush slid down his throat, so cold, so wet, and he retched.

"That's better." She wrenched his head down to look in his eyes, hers wide and manic, pissholes in soot. "Who's a good boy then? Candy Boy."

* * *

Karl couldn't stand the instructions any longer. Her voice came out of a hidden speaker, arrowing straight into his ears. Monotone. Bland. Order after order.

"You will use the candy cane."

"You will slice your wrist."

"You will bleed out."

"You will die."

Laughter.

"Think of the release."

"No more raw meat."

"No more shitting and wetting yourself."

He could move fine now and had tried to kick her the first time he'd been able to raise a leg, but she'd remained just outside his reach, pushing the trolley towards him and standing there, fingers to her temples, smiling at him willingly eating that disgusting shite she brought in. She was there now, in her stupid nightie, at the back of the room, a montage of grotesque images on the plaster at her rear. He forked in the meat while she mimed the words coming out of the speaker.

"Kill yourself."

"You can stop this if you really want to."

"The candy cane, it's right there, within reach. It's the end."

It was, on a pedestal to his left, and had been for a while. There was a blade on the end of it, and it gleamed, the rest of it a normal cane, white-and-pink stripes. He could take hold of it and do what she wanted, and he might if the orders didn't stop. They were driving him insane.

She pushed a button on the wall, and the commands mercifully ceased.

"That's an animal's testicle you're eating, that is, all mushed up."

He coughed, heaving, and spat the food on the floor. "Why are you doing this to me?" It came out as a wail. Pitiful.

"You *know* why."

She prodded the button, and her recorded voice droned on.

Sister Leeanne, Felicity Gray, or whoever the fuck she was, walked out, giggling, the cadence of it chilling him to the core.

* * *

The next day, Sister Leeanne practised karate on him. He was her fight dummy, she said, like the one on the YouTube video. The kicks and chops she landed on him hurt until they didn't anymore, his body going numb, his mind drifting elsewhere, his soul floating above him, so he watched it without being attached to the proceedings.

His nose bled. His ribs cracked. Bruises clouded his once white skin.

When she left, muttering, "That'll teach you, Dillon!", he closed his eyes.

The chants set up their rhythmic orders.

Karl reached for the candy cane.

CHAPTER TWO

Bethany and Mike sat in the café at the retail park, using their lunch break to grab a quick drink to warm them up. They'd been tromping around Shadwell, looking for some bloke who'd fleeced an old woman out of her life savings. The poor love hadn't been the only one — several had had their money whipped out from under their noses — and the bastard had gone to ground.

Mike munched on a slice of carrot cake, while she'd opted for chocolate. The coffee was working wonders, and it was nice to take a moment to breathe. The place was crowded with people buying last-minute gifts, carrier bags parked around feet, the air thick with the scent of cinnamon from the Christmas-tree-shaped biscuits on offer.

"What a year, eh?" she said, leaning back.

"That's one way of putting it." Mike smiled. "Here's hoping we get to spend Christmas at home. I'm really looking forward to it."

In a way, Bethany was, too, although celebrating Yuletide without Vinny had been hard last time. No thoughtful presents from him waited under her tree, which was a miniature fibre-optic she'd stuck on the living room windowsill as a nod to the festive season. A token to acknowledge it. She mainly needed the break, a chance to rest without haring around trying to catch people who had a mind to commit the worst of crimes.

"Going to your mum's, aren't you?" she said.

"Yeah, and the offer still stands if you change your mind and want to come, too."

She didn't. "No, I'm better off on my own, but thanks again." She filled her mouth with cake to stop herself waffling on about how she really felt. Lost. Melancholy. Wishing Vinny was here. How she missed him so much at times it was as though she had an actual hole inside her, yawning, pushing against her innards.

"I'm glad that old lady who was scammed has family," he said. "Imagine her being by herself at Christmas after what's just happened. I don't know how that bloke can live with himself."

"Hmm."

Mrs Watson was ninety and as sweet as anything. She'd planned to leave her money to her kids, who both had huge mortgages, going to her grave knowing she'd done them a favour by saving all her spare cash over the years, the interest mounting up into a hefty sum. Now, she was broke — in more ways than one.

"I hope this doesn't end up killing her," Bethany said. "The shock and upset of it."

"That'd be awful. He has a lot to answer for. I bet he's swanned off somewhere to spend it. I totted up the amount he's stolen from various people. Over a million."

"I thought it had to be something like that."

Bethany stared out of the window. A tramp sat on the snowy ground, leaning against a lamppost, his coat so thin it couldn't be keeping the chill out. The bloody thing was too big for him, his rickety frame shrouded by so much fabric. He had to be about seventy, with his long white beard and lank, greasy hair that settled on his shoulders.

"Look at that poor sod there," she said. "It shouldn't have to come to this. An elderly man, out on the streets, hoping someone will come out of here and give him some cash. I'll buy him a coffee and a sandwich."

They got up, and Bethany made the purchase, then led the way outside. Christ, it was bitter cold, the air a bone-chilling miasma of icy, heavy mist, tightening her lungs. She approached the man and hunkered down, handing him the food and drink.

"Do you go to the shelter?" she asked.

"Thank you." He cradled his blue-tipped fingers around the hot cup. "Warehouse. People in the shelter nick your shit."

"Do you have a blanket?"

"Nope." He shrugged. "I'm used to it, the cold."

Her heart panged. "Stay there. I'll be right back."

She legged it into the camping shop and returned with her purchases — a lightweight backpack with a metal frame, a thick jacket, a sleeping bag used by people who climbed Everest, and a flask so he could at least get water from a public loo or whatever and carry it around with him.

"What's that for?" he asked, turning his rheumy eyes up to her.

"A present." She handed him her card. "If you need help, ring me, and I'll put you in touch with the relevant people."

He stared down at it, squinting. "A copper."

She nodded.

"I'll be buggered," he said. "Thank you very much."

"What's your name?" she asked.

"Curmudgeon."

"That a nickname?"

"It's the only one I go by. Whoever I was before is long gone." He placed the coffee down, slid into the jacket, and put the rolled-up sleeping bag in the backpack. "Blimey, that's a good 'un. I'll have to use the backpack as a pillow. Like I said, shit gets nicked."

Bethany walked away, shoulders slumped. Had she done enough? Should she have contacted the council to see if they had a flat for him? She turned back and called out to him, "Do you want me to help get you off the streets?"

He laughed, showing gaps between his teeth. "That'd be like turfing me out of my own home. I'm fine where I am."

She got in the car, Mike beside her, and stared out of the windscreen.

"That was a nice thing to do," he said.

"There's him out here in the fucking snow, and Mrs Watson at home, her purse lighter, granted, but she's safe and warm. The differences in the lives of two old people are staggering."

"But he doesn't want it any different."

She started the engine. "Hmm. It's still going to bother me, though."

"But he'll be warmer tonight, thanks to you."

"I s'pose."

She drove off, glancing in her rearview. Curmudgeon munched on his sandwich.

"Poor bastard," she muttered.

Her phone rang, and she indicated to her pocket for Mike to get it out and answer it for her. She'd never got to grips with hands-free. "Stick it on speaker, will you?"

"It's Rob," he said.

"Ah, the wonder of the front desk. Let's see what he wants then."

Mike swiped to answer and set it to loudspeaker. "Mike here. Beth's driving."

"Hi, you two." Rob cleared his throat. Sighed.

"Bad news, I take it?" Bethany asked.

"A body."

"Oh, for fuck's sake! Of all the times to discover one!" *Bang goes our Christmas break.*

"Sorry," Rob said.

"Not your fault." She gripped the steering wheel tighter. "Where?"

"Propped up against a headstone in the cemetery. Well, one of them tombs, the stone sort."

"What?" She blew out a breath. "Okay. Do we have a name?"

"Karl Hartley. Want me to pass that on to Fran and Leona?"

"Please."

"Isabelle's on her way. You'll need plot twelve. It's one of the first graves there, beside the church. The tomb's about two hundred years old apparently."

Why he thought she needed a history lesson, she didn't know. She felt a bitch for her thoughts and said cheerily, "Thanks, Rob. Chat soon."

Mike ended the call. "Mum said she bets she won't see me this Christmas. She had a feeling about it."

"Well, we'll just have to get a move on and wrap this up quickly, won't we."

"Inside a few days?"

"Yep, and if all is quiet and we're getting nowhere by Christmas Eve, we'll still take it off. I don't want Fran working it. She's got her kiddie to make memories with."

That had been on her mind a lot lately. While Fran had chosen her profession, the amount of time her job took her away from her child bothered Bethany. If she could help in that regard, she would.

She headed for the cemetery, a massive place with thousands of dead resting there. The church had been around for five hundred years and was undergoing external renovations, the spire encased in scaffolding that marred the beauty of it. She'd learnt that bit of info from *The Shadwell Herald*, not Rob.

She parked up on the road behind a SOCO van, and they got out, the top of the tent visible over the stone perimeter wall.

Bethany entered via the black, rusty iron gate. Tory Yates was on the other side with the log. Bethany and Mike said their hellos and signed in, put on protective clothing from the plastic bag beside Tory, and then walked along the path. SOCOs flitted about between old, crumbling headstones, the snow sullied by their footprints, squashed grass peering through. The tent flap drew across, and Isabelle poked her head out, face mask lowered.

"Ah, there you are." She shook her head. "This one's . . . horrible. Always seems more rotten at this time of year."

"It does." What with meeting Curmudgeon and now this, the season that was supposed to be jolly was turning into the most *un*-jolly.

Bethany and Mike entered the tent, and she caught her breath. The body, naked, sat against the grey tomb, legs out straight and together, hand palms up, resting on his thighs. His skin, mottled with hundreds of bruises, appeared as a plethora of storm clouds, dark, purple, black and burgundy. Fresh. The inner end of one of his ribs pressed the flesh from beneath to create a lump where it was undoubtedly broken. She studied the head. Tipped back, throat exposed, the Adam's apple a ripe plum in the slender column.

Karl was thin, a body starved of food over a long period of time, or perhaps he was anorexic. Blood coated his face from the nose downwards, and it had dribbled under his chin. Oedema puffed up the area around his bulging eyes, and it was so clear he'd been beaten up. His arm, though . . .

She winced. Had he cut it himself? Or had whoever attacked him done it? Presley, the ME, would tell them once he got here. It'd be something to do with the angle of the slice that'd determine what had happened. That slice went from inner elbow to wrist, the skin parted, like an open handbag, as though a zip had formally kept it together. Flesh, yellow fat, muscles and bone were exposed. Whoever had made the wound had dug deep at the elbow end, the knife extremely sharp. This wasn't the usual shallow incision of a person committing suicide. No attempt marks, where they'd cut a few times, losing their bottle before going for the finale. This was a definite action.

"Well, Merry Christmas, ya filthy animals," Mike said.

"You like the *Home Alone* films, too, then?" Isabelle laughed. "I mean, I wanted a decent present, but this one's taking the piss."

Bethany smiled at the gallows humour. If they didn't joke sometimes, they'd go mad. Being presented with such a wicked end to a life was harrowing. One day they might wallow in the tragedy of that, sad and morose, but on others, like today, they brushed it off.

"One family is going to hate Christmas for the rest of their lives," Bethany said. "Um, how do we know his name?" She glanced about for signs of ID.

"Well, that's where it gets interesting." Isabelle beckoned. "Come here."

Bethany and Mike followed her, treading in a narrow path already made in the snow. Round the side of the tomb, a stack of clothing had been folded neatly and placed on a square of heavy-duty, transparent plastic sheeting. Beside it was a piece of paper in a zipped sandwich bag. Bethany went down on her haunches to read what was on it.

KARL HARTLEY. A QUARTER OF A CENTURY. HOMELESS FILTH.

She stood and frowned. "That's a bit harsh, calling him filth."

"Some people think of the homeless like rats," Isabelle said. "Vermin on our streets."

"We saw an old boy today," Mike said. "He seems to like the life."

"Can't say I'd be fond of kipping on the pavement." Isabelle shivered. "And in this weather . . ."

"I know. Awful." Bethany sighed. "So, at least we have something to go on." She led the way back to the front of the tomb. "The question is, how did the killer know his name if he's homeless? And why was he beaten up and left here in the buff?"

"Don't ask me. That's your area of expertise." Isabelle smirked.

"Was this path already made when you got here?" Bethany asked.

"Yes. And the tramping down of snow around him. We took photos before we put the tent up, before we disturbed the scene. As you can see, we've fucked it now." Isabelle walked over to the corner where a halogen stood on a pole.

She switched it on, and the light gave the snow a bright tint. "That's better. Bloody trees out there overhanging the tent makes for gloom."

Bethany turned at the tent flap being eased open, and Presley appeared in the gap.

"Afternoon," he said. "Bit of a spooky place. Never did like cemeteries."

"Odd, seeing as all the people you work on usually end up in one." Isabelle guffawed. "This has been made to look like a suicide, by the way."

"I'll be the judge of that." Presley stomped over the unmarked snow. "One deep slice. Someone was determined."

"I'm going with a killer," Bethany said. "There's his clothes and a note down the side. With no blood around him, he can't have killed himself here."

Presley knelt beside Karl and peered at the arm. "It's consistent with him doing it himself."

Bethany frowned.

Mike did the same. "So he offed himself, and someone found him and brought him here? Another homeless person?"

Bethany thought about Curmudgeon and what he'd said about people stealing. Could Karl have gotten into a fight over his belongings, then topped himself for whatever reason? Where had he got the knife from? Or did he own one for protection? Did he have any other possessions? If so, where were they?

"He's stiff as a board." Presley riffled about in his bag. "The weather isn't helping. Rigor is just starting, so he's been dead for over six hours. It lasts from eight to twelve. Seven or eight this morning is my guess, then he'd have to be brought here without the person being seen doing it."

"We'll have to go and speak to the vicar or whoever," Bethany said. "Is that who found him?"

"Yep." Isabelle nodded. "He's gone into the church."

"Righty-oh. Come on, Mike."

Presley stood and took his clipboard out and got on with sketching Karl's position. Isabelle walked out with them and spoke to a SOCO. Bethany led the way farther up the path and entered the church via a large, arched wooden doorway. She stepped into a porch, the aisle ahead. At the end, in front of the altar, a man knelt, praying. Candles lit the area around him, but otherwise, with minimal light coming in through the stained glass windows, the place was pretty dingy.

She strode along the burgundy carpet runner that filled the aisle, her footfalls muffled but still audible. Mike's thudded behind her, and she came to a stop just as the man rose and turned to face them. His black trousers and jumper over a black shirt with a white dog collar at the neck pronounced him as the bloke they needed to speak to. He was younger than she'd expected, probably about thirty.

Bethany brandished her ID and introduced them. "And your name is?"

"Father Oswald."

"Oswald what, sir?" Bethany smiled to put him at ease. The poor fucker must have had one hell of a fright.

"Nichols. Would you like some tea?"

"Do you have coffee?" Cheeky of her, but if you didn't ask, you didn't get.

"Of course. I have a small office here. Let's go in there."

He guided them to the right, past a gaudy statue of Mary in her blue-and-white robes, and through a doorway to a cosy room with a sofa, kitchenette and a desk. Coffee made, they sat, Oswald behind his desk.

"What time did you come here this morning?" Bethany asked.

"I always arrive by ten."

"So did you come via the gate?"

He nodded. "Yes. I was distracted and didn't spot him. I came in here and dealt with some paperwork for the Women's Institute Christmas bazaar, plus had a conversation on the phone with a lady who's having problems at home. The morning sped by, and with no visitors to the church, it was a quiet one. I stepped out for a late lunch at home and, on the way down the path, I caught a glimpse of him. He stuck out against the snow and the light colour of the tomb. All those bruises . . ." He shuddered.

"Did you notice if there were footsteps in the snow that weren't yours?"

"I did but assumed someone had come to lay flowers, except the footsteps didn't go all the way up the path and round past the church to the other burial plots at the back. They went in a straight line beside mine from the gate then veered to the right, to the tomb. There was quite a bit of trampling down in that area, then another set where the person came back and left the same way."

Bethany would study the photos to get a better idea, but for now, his description had told her the person who'd delivered the body had possibly been the first to tread on the fresh snow that had fallen overnight.

"Okay," she said. "What did you do when you saw the body?"

"Well, apart from having a massive shock, I phoned the police on my mobile and stayed exactly where I was — not for the want of trying to move, mind you. I *couldn't* move."

"Shock manifests in many ways. What then?"

"The police lady in uniform arrived, then the others with the tent. I came inside after talking to a woman called Isabelle. She said you'd come soon. I prayed for the poor soul. Why did he do that to himself?"

"We don't know that yet," she said then took a sip of coffee. "Do you live locally?"

He nodded. "Yes, just over the road there, opposite actually, which is a bit chilling."

"Did you see anyone hanging around this morning?"

"No, my kitchen's out the back, and I ate my breakfast there."

After a general chat, where Oswald was much calmer, Bethany and Mike left. They needed to nip to the station and find out the next of kin.

That was a visit she didn't want to make in a hurry.

CHAPTER THREE

"I really wish you weren't here," Mother said.

Leeanne stared at her, wishing she wasn't here either. Other children had lovely mummies, she'd seen them in the school playground, all smiles and cuddles when picking their kids up. Leeanne had no one to do that to her. She walked home by herself, and once, the teacher had asked her why. Leeanne couldn't say her mother didn't want to, that Leeanne was a burden, and the less Mother had to do with her, the better. That would cause trouble, and she wasn't allowed to do that. No one must know what it was like at home.

"I should have aborted you."

How many times had Leeanne heard that? She didn't even know what it meant. Mother said some strange things at times, stuff that was hard to understand, but if Leeanne dared to ask for an explanation, she'd get a punch in the head.

"Maybe I should shove you into foster care."

Leeanne didn't know what that was either. Was it something to do with the cans Mother sometimes drank? They had Foster's on them.

"Go to the caravan."

Leeanne grabbed Mr Teddy and walked out of the house, into the garden. The drive at the side led to the grass, and the quaint little caravan sat at the back beneath the canopy of trees. The house was old, a nunnery once upon a time, and Mother had been given it by the nun they used to live with.

She climbed up the wooden steps and smiled at the painted flowers on the side of the caravan. It was a Romany effort, so pretty, and gifted to the nun by a grateful fortune teller upon her death. It served as Leeanne's bolt-hole, somewhere she was safe, providing Mother didn't come out there.

Inside, she sat on the U-shaped seating to the left which also turned into a big bed. The cushions on it were old and floral, the material a bit coarse. She rested on her side and snuggled beneath the patchwork quilt the fortune teller had crafted in between telling people their futures. The nun had told Leeanne many a story about the Romany, ones that came to life in her head, a magical time out on the road, free of burdens.

She missed the nun.

Sister Maggie James, her name was, an old lady who'd befriended Mother when she'd first had Leeanne. Maggie had told Leeanne all about how she'd met Mother, who'd walked up the drive with an hours-old Leeanne placed inside a carrier bag. Maggie had taken them in, caring for them, feeding Leeanne and bringing her up.

Until she'd died.

Leeanne scrunched her eyes closed and shoved her thumb in her mouth. She didn't like remembering that day. Seeing what she'd seen, losing the only person who'd cared for her.

She got up on her knees and looked out of the window towards the house. The dark-grey stones and leaded windows, all except one in the middle, which was stained glass, should have comforted her, but they didn't anymore. Not when Maggie wasn't in there. Life without her was cruel. Wicked. It gave Leeanne nightmares. Mother had always been mean to her, doing it when Maggie wasn't around, but now she was mean all the time.

An image of Maggie came into Leeanne's head. She smiled, tears stinging. Maggie had said she'd always be with Leeanne, no matter what, but she'd lied. She'd let herself be killed six months after signing her house over to Mother.

Poison, Mother was, and one day, when she was bigger, Leeanne was going to do to her what she'd helped do to the beloved Maggie. Then the house would be hers.

* * *

There was a man who regularly came to Maggie's — 'filth' Mother had called him at first, but Maggie said that wasn't his name, it was Dillon. Maggie fed him and gave him a bed for the night sometimes, so he didn't have to kip out on the street. While Maggie and Mother were fast asleep, Dillon liked to visit Leeanne's bedroom.

His weight always dipped the mattress.

His breath was always hot on her cheek.

His chest always pressed onto her face when he —

* * *

Leeanne was drawing another picture on the holding room wall. These images came back to her from a childhood of confusion, where she'd dreamt of the Devil coming to take Dillon and Mother away, secreting them in his Hell house, torturing them endlessly and then killing them. The Devil held their still-pulsing hearts in his hands, blood dripping, and ripped a hole in their stomachs, letting everything inside tumble out and dangle. Drawing soothed her and gave her peace, as did Maggie's soft white nightie and comfortable slippers.

She thought about this morning when she'd dropped Karl off at the church and how cold it had been, that part of Shadwell devoid of people, all the curtains in the houses opposite closed, shutting off the sight of the frost-bitten weather. How lucky she'd been, to park up, take him out of the passenger seat where she'd propped him, and carry him to the tomb. He'd weighed nothing much, but even if he had, it didn't matter. She was strong, karate saw to that. She'd left his clothes, a stinking pile, and a note so whoever found him could take his manky body back to the mother who'd kicked him out.

Tonight, she'd put on Maggie's habit again, and go and find another Dillon. All those homeless people were just the same. Dirty, perverted bastards, even the women.

There'd been a time, back in the day, when Leeanne had lived in fear, her nerves constantly ragged. She'd endured

Mother's bullying until some time after her eighteenth, then snapped. Years had passed with her feeling content, until she'd seen a stack of candy canes in a shop window a little while ago and it had brought it all back.

Now, her mind had turned, and she knew it, but there wasn't anything she could do about it. Nor did she want to. The suppressed rage had to go somewhere. She so badly wanted to be Felicity Gray, but Leeanne Paling spoke louder, and she obeyed that voice.

She placed her charcoal down and admired her picture of Karl strapped to the wooden pole. Face bloodied. Skin bruised.

He deserved that. They all did.

She pressed her fingers to her temples and turned her hands one way, then the other. Tipped her head and licked Karl's likeness. He tasted bad.

She wondered what the next one would taste like. Sour. Evil.

"This is wrong," Stout Farmer said inside her head.

She ignored him, went upstairs to her bedroom and switched on the computer. She spoke into the microphone, recording a new set of orders, then repeated them to herself over and over, so she'd know them off by heart.

She stroked her candy cane, one she'd made out of metal and painted, then varnished. It had a pointed tip on the long end, something that cut deep. It reminded her of another time, that cane, but she didn't want to think about it at the moment. It brought back such terrible memories. The peppermint taste of it. The sugary sweetness. What had come after she'd sucked on the original one had changed her forever. Turned her into . . . this.

She stood in front of her vanity mirror and added more black eyeshadow. She looked like Maggie had at the end, eyes sunken, cheekbones sticking out. If she became Maggie and lured in the Dillons, everything would be okay.

Wouldn't it?

CHAPTER FOUR

Bethany stood in front of the whiteboards and faced the incident room. "Okay, what have you got for me?"

Fran pulled her notebook towards her. "Karl Hartley, twenty-five, left home at fifteen. Mother alive, father unknown."

"*Left* home?"

"Well, according to his mother, he said he didn't want to live with her anymore and walked out."

"Didn't she report him as missing?"

"No, she didn't say anything about it until the school rang her after he hadn't been there for a fortnight."

Bethany couldn't wrap her head around that. "Was a search made for him?"

"This happened twenty miles away in Campford. The police there looked out for him, did a bit of work talking to his friends — he only had two — but dropped it after it was clear he wasn't going to return. Kids voluntarily leave home all the time, and if they don't want to be found, then they're not."

"I know, but fifteen . . . How did the mother seem?"

"She slurred quite a bit over the phone — I'd say she had a bevvy or two inside her. She didn't seem all that bothered, to be honest."

"Bitch. Well, I'm not leaving her to the Campford police. We'll go and see her. Was there anything said by the school?"

"That Karl was a loner, didn't mix well. They didn't know anything about his home life. He was a private child."

"Right. What's her address?"

Fran gave it. "As Karl isn't on any social media, shall we go back to Mrs Watson's money theft case?"

"Please, but one of you needs to check CCTV on the roads leading to the church."

"I'll do that," Leona said.

Bethany gestured to Mike, and they got on the road. It didn't take long to get to Campford, a small town that had probably been a village once but had now expanded on the outskirts, with an explosion of housing estates going up on the perimeter as well as a retail park with the usual Burger King, KFC, Next, B&Q and the like. The population was ever-growing, and the need for homes swallowing up the countryside.

Eloise Hartley lived at thirteen Valour Street, which was a bit of a dive. The houses were worse for wear, although some were having fake brick cladding put on the outside and new windows fitted. The council had clearly stepped up to tidy them. Eloise's hadn't been done yet, the pebbledash covered in mould from the bottom, up to beneath the front window.

Bethany knocked, and Mike stood beside her on the ridged cement path.

The door swung open, and a woman stood in the frame, all saggy jowls and wrinkled skin, although she wasn't old. The world hadn't treated her kindly, or maybe it was the alcohol inside the huge gin glass she clutched that had ravaged her appearance. Her hair, dyed a lurid shade of red, didn't match her black eyebrows.

"Yeah?" she said.

Bethany showed her ID. "DI Bethany Smith, and this is DS Mike Wilkins. My colleague spoke to you earlier today about your son, Karl. We need to come in."

"I don't want to hear anything about that little bastard."

Christ. "Well, you're going to have to — unless you want to discuss it on your doorstep?"

Eloise glanced about, peering between Bethany and Mike. Bethany turned around. A woman had come out opposite, shovelling snow off her path, staring over.

"Hmm, inside then," Eloise said, "so Nosy Knickers doesn't get an inkling."

She wandered off down the hall, weaving, and Bethany followed, leaving Mike to shut the door. In a living room crowded with furniture, dust covering all surfaces, Bethany remained by the entrance with Mike. Eloise sat on the sofa — the only seat that wasn't covered in magazines. If Karl had lived here like this, no wonder he'd walked out.

"Come on then," Eloise barked, "less avvit." She gulped down some of her drink. "What's he done? Got himself in the nick, has he?"

"Why did your son leave home?" Bethany asked.

Eloise shrugged. "Said he didn't want to live here no more. Took a rucksack and fucked off."

"Did you have a row prior to this?"

Eloise pursed her lips. "Well, he was a wrong 'un. I'd had a word with him about nicking a phone off a kid at school, didn't I. Parental responsibility and all that. He'd only gone and sold the bleedin' thing, then gave the money to some twat in his class."

"Was the 'word' you had with him heated?"

"I might have raised my voice a bit, but it doesn't mean I'm in the wrong. He walked out, end of. He wasn't long off sixteen, give or take a month or two, so there was nothing I could do about it anyway."

"Why didn't you report him as missing?"

"Because he wasn't missing. Left of his own accordion."

"Accord. Right. Could he have gone to his father's?"

She laughed. "Even *I* don't know who that is."

Lovely. "Did you have any contact with him between then and now?"

"Nope."

"So no silent calls over the years, where he'd maybe rung you and changed his mind about speaking?"

"I've had a few heavy-breathing ones, but that'll be old Cecil, the pervert."

"Who is Cecil?"

"Just the weirdo at the end of the street. He's harmless." Eloise shrugged. "So what are you here for?"

Seeing as the woman had been blunt about Karl, Bethany didn't care about delivering the news bluntly either. "Your son was found dead this afternoon."

The woman widened her eyes. "And what do you want *me* to do about that?"

"Burying him would be a start."

"Well, you can fuck right off on that one. He cut himself off from me, and anyway, where am I going to get the money from to bury him? My customers are few and far between these days."

"Customers?"

"The least you know about that, the better." She winked. "Know what I mean?"

Bethany didn't have time to talk to her about the pitfalls of prostitution, if that was what Eloise was on about. "Do Karl's friends still live in Campford?"

"How am I meant to bloody know?"

"Thank you for your time." If Bethany didn't get out of the house, she'd say something she'd regret. She walked out and, while waiting for Mike in the car, who'd got caught up talking on the pisshead's doorstep, she rang Fran. "Can you give me the names and addresses of the friends mentioned in the police report from when Karl left home? Sorry, I should have brought them with me."

Fran gave them to her, and Bethany scribbled the info down.

"Okay, we're going to visit them now. Karl's mother was drunk and about as much use as a cement sponge."

"Didn't think she'd be any cop."

Bethany said goodbye and slipped her phone away, turning to Mike when he got in. "What the chuff did she have to say?"

"That Karl had told her, during their 'word', that he'd pinched the phone because he was being bullied and needed to give some kid the money after selling it."

"Interesting. Did she say who the kid was?"

"She didn't know but reckoned it was a lie on Karl's part. You know, a story to get himself out of trouble."

"I feel for the kid he was. We'll go and find his friends now. They still live here, thank goodness. Satnav time." She plugged in the first address and set off, imagining Karl as a teen, picked on at school and not cared for properly at home. What was the matter with some parents?

The sat nav directed her to one of the newer estates, situated behind the retail park. The builds appear to have mainly two or three bedrooms, cookie-cutter and so fragile-looking that a good wind might knock them over. She parked outside one and checked the man's name. On the doorstep, Mike pressed the bell, and they waited. The bloke might not be in, seeing as it wasn't clocking-off time yet.

A male answered, built like a brick shithouse, brawn packed on from obvious hours at the gym. The cords in his neck stood out, and he seemed menacing, a no-nonsense aura wafting around him.

He squinted.

"Richard Vickham? DI Bethany Smith and DS Wilkins." She held up her ID. "We're here to ask a few questions about a friend of yours. Karl Hartley."

"Blimey, that's a blast from the past. Come in." He pushed the door wider and stepped back to allow them to pass. In the kitchen, he said, "What's he been doing all these years then?"

"From what we can gather, he's been homeless."

"Bloody hell, that's not good. Where did he end up?" He pointed at the kettle. "Want a drink?"

"No, thank you. He moved to Shadwell. We just need some idea of him, or rather who he was. His mother . . . wasn't much help."

"Oh, that old bitch. Alcoholic. Free with her favours, if you catch my drift. She didn't care about Karl one bit. I went round there once as a kid. Never again. She was off her face, shouting at us to keep the noise down. All we were doing was our homework."

Dreadful creature. "So what can you tell us about him?"

"He never said much about his home life, but I could see it wasn't great. We were mates, but not best mates, know what I mean? Like, we hung out a couple of times but mainly just said hello and had a chat at break. Everyone took the piss out of him, and one kid used to bully him. Can't remember his name, though."

"Did it surprise you when Karl left home?"

"Yes and no. Yes, because I didn't think he had the bottle, and no, because I wouldn't want to have a mum like that and couldn't blame him for walking out. I spoke to the police just after he went — well, a fortnight later, but nothing came of it. I've often wondered what he got up to and whether he ended up making a decent life for himself."

"We're not sure what happened between him leaving home and now, but it seems he was on the streets." She wasn't about to tell him a note at the scene had implied so. "I'm sorry to say he was found dead this morning. We suspect it's murder, although it could be ruled as a suicide."

"What? Fuck me . . . Did he get in with a bad lot or something? Drugs?"

"Toxicology from the post-mortem will tell us that. Is there anything else you can remember that might help us?"

He shook his head.

"Okay, thank you for your time. I'll leave you my card in case you recall something." She handed it over.

In the car, she let out a sigh.

"Is it just me, or did that kid have a shit time of it, before *and* after he'd left home?" Mike said.

"Sounds like he's one of life's discarded. Mother's an alchie, a dad he never knew, there's a bully at school, then he buggers off because he can't stand it, and ten years pass with him doing God knows what. Then he winds up dead. There's no job record, Fran has been through all that, so did he make it to Shadwell and then just roam about, begging? If he did, there's no record of him being arrested for it. We're going to have to visit the shelter as well, see what they know of him, if anything."

She sorted the sat nav and drove to the next address. A blond man was getting out of a blue Mini in the drive, so they collared him there. Sadly, he had nothing to offer, really, a similar statement to what Richard Vickham had given, so they returned to Shadwell, where she parked outside the shelter.

The sign, A HELPING HAND, was affixed to the one-storey brick building above racing-green, double doors with glass in the top that reminded her of a community centre. Inside, a corridor had gleaming floor tiles, and to the right, another set of double doors, this time grey. Beyond, in a large hall, narrow beds with blue, plastic-covered mattresses, like those in the holding cells, stood either side, about forty in all. A pillow and a rolled-up blanket sat at the foot of each.

A blonde woman poked her head out of a doorway to the left. "Can I help you?"

Bethany took out her ID and introduced them. "Your name?"

"Sandy Cossar."

"I realise you have many people coming through, but I'm hoping that one man in particular might have been a regular. Karl Hartley."

"Oh, yes, he used to stay here a couple of times a week until recently. I haven't seen him for a while. There was a spat about his holdall — he said someone stole something out of it."

Him nicking the phone at school. Some would say that's karma . . . "Right. When was the last time you saw him?"

"Here? I can tell you the exact date from the log. But more recently, I saw him with Curmudgeon — don't ask, he won't answer to any other name. Won't give his real one either. They were on their way to the warehouse when I was locking up here for the night. We take it in turns to do the night shifts so someone's always on hand inside."

"I know Curmudgeon," Bethany said, wondering why, in all the years she'd lived in Shadwell, she'd never encountered him before, and today, she'd met him, plus he'd been mentioned now. "He said he doesn't bother with the shelter but uses the warehouse. Do you know where that is?"

"Yes, it's the empty one behind here. If you walk down the alley at the side, you'll see it. It's made of metal; you know the type I mean?"

Bethany nodded. "You mentioned a log . . ."

Sandy beckoned them into the room she was hanging out of. "Here." She pointed to a desk with a black, leather-bound ledger on it. "Everyone must sign in if they're lucky enough to get a spot — fire regulations, even though most of them give false names. People will start arriving soon. They're allowed in from six onwards until eight in the morning. They get a meal at seven at night, then a bacon roll, plus a cuppa, before they leave."

"How do you choose who gets in?"

"First come, first served, although they know they mustn't camp outside all day until six. Absolutely no queuing until five-forty-five. I hate sending the others away. We only have forty-eight beds, and going by our log, there are over two hundred homeless that we're aware of."

That was a lot of people, and heartbreaking to hear. "Who funds this place?"

"It's a charity, so we rely on donations, which is why we can't do anything with the warehouse — the money doesn't stretch to that, but it *would* be handy to use the building if we could get more funding. It's big enough that it would help the other one hundred-odd we can't put up. It comes with the lease of this place, and we're not supposed to allow anyone in there unsupervised, but the door hasn't got a lock, so we turn a blind eye . . ."

They leave it open on purpose. "I understand, especially in this weather."

"Exactly. About twenty people use it, five or six of them at a time, so it's not like it's crammed. Karl is one of them, and Curmudgeon . . . well, you could say he runs it. Only lets certain people in. He keeps the troublemakers out. That man has been homeless forever, and prefers to be, so he kind of helps us, although where he goes during the day I wouldn't know. He's the only one who gets meals even when he's not in the actual shelter. It's payment for how he persuades the younger homeless to find more permanent places and employment, or to go home."

"That didn't work for Karl then."

"No, he's much like Curmudgeon. Karl has never entertained trying to better himself. He walks miles every day around Shadwell and has done since he arrived ten years ago. I was here when he rolled up for the first time. A teenager. Sixteen, he said."

"He was actually fifteen and had left home after a row. Do you know of anyone who might be upset with him?"

"No. God, the poor lad. The man who took Karl's possession hasn't been seen since, otherwise I'd say him. He was possibly just passing through."

"Sorry to break this news, but his body was found today."

Sandy dropped into her desk chair, face paling, tears spilling. "W-what?"

Bethany didn't have the heart to explain exactly what had happened to him, no one needed that visual, so she went with the basics. "Did he ever confide in you about suicide?"

"No." Sandy shook her head vehemently. "I can't believe this. Karl was happy despite his situation. It doesn't make sense."

"I don't mean to push you when you've had a shock, but can you check the log now? We really need at least one point of reference to know where he was recently, then we can work from there."

Sandy flipped back a few pages and then moved her finger down a column of names. "Here. Fifteenth of October."

"Thanks."

With a printout of all the homeless people Sandy knew, Bethany and Mike returned to the car. As she reversed out of the spot, the first of the homeless arrived and stood in an orderly line outside the shelter.

Bethany drove off, her heart cracking. She *had* to help these people.

At the station, she contacted *The Shadwell Herald — not* that dick, Phillip Uxbridge, but Angela Hill, the editor. Bethany idly wondered if she was related to Tammy, one of the PCs, then dismissed it. Tammy had come up here with her boyfriend, Charlie, from Bicester, and hadn't mentioned having family this way.

Angela agreed to write a piece about the homeless and would look into raising funds. Bethany wanted that warehouse operational. The idea of over one hundred and fifty lost souls living rough was intolerable. She just wished she'd known about it sooner. Leading a privileged life with her head stuck into crime wasn't an excuse. She should have been more interested in her community.

She nodded to herself, happy she had another goal to keep her from thinking about Vinny too much. He'd be proud of her for this, and she'd show him, wherever he was, what she could do. Later, they'd go to the warehouse and see if Curmudgeon would speak to them. For now, she sent Fran and Leona home and took Mike out to dinner. All right, it was pub grub, but it was better than anything the shelter lot were having.

So many things to be grateful for.

CHAPTER FIVE

Sister Leeanne walked over the high street pavement that had been gritted, the snow stamped away by numerous feet throughout the day. Frost sparkled on it, though, and she'd bet black ice waited, hidden, ready to send her on her arse, the snide bastard. People darted here and there, bags full of presents they'd have to wrap up, rushing around and taking advantage of the shops being open later than usual.

It was six-thirty, and she'd already walked past her target several times, some bloke dossing in the doorway of the Vodafone shop that had shut its doors at five-thirty. She'd been careful of any cameras. Head bent, *his* scarf over the lower half of her face, Maggie's habit flowing, she dropped a leaflet she'd designed and printed off. It fluttered to land over his inappropriate shoes, a paper blanket that would do nothing to warm his toes. She walked on, slowly, waiting, waiting for—

"Hold up!" he said.

She smiled and continued on, rounding the corner where the road had a park on one side behind the shops and a row of houses on the other. She'd left her car there earlier, then cut across the park so she could walk up the high street from the other end.

"Hold up," he said again, closer now.

She spun to face him, her heart thudding with excitement, and peered at the skinny wanker who'd fallen for her false promises of a safe place to live with the nuns. It was hard not to chuckle.

"Oh, child." She reached out and touched his shoulder, unable to see his face clearly, the darkness shadowing it. She inwardly cringed at the contact. "God has brought you to me."

"Nah, it was your leaflet, innit."

Oh. He was one of *those*. A chav.

He didn't talk like Dillon. She was momentarily confused.

"God made you read it. Will you come with me?" she asked. "Christmas is no time for you to be alone."

"Yeah, cheers, I'm fucking starving."

What a charmer.

She led him to her car, hand clamped to his elbow, which was bony beneath the thin fabric of his fleece jacket. "Here, let's get you inside."

She opened the door, and he climbed in, rubbing his dirty hands, his nails thick with a layer of grime. Gliding around to the driver's side, she joined him, almost gagging on his stench.

Just like Dillon at the start . . .

Anger burbled, and she revved the engine, the heater exacerbating his smell.

"A shower first, I think," she said, speeding off. "Tell me about yourself."

He yabbered on about his wife and how she'd kicked him out after he'd got her best friend pregnant. Life wasn't fair, he said, how it kicked you in the teeth. She glanced across at him, alarmed to see he didn't *have* many, so life had certainly kicked him a fair few times.

"Oh, that's dreadful," she said. "And you have a child, you say."

I bet she wasn't put in a carrier bag at birth and carried around.

Hatred for Mother pushed Leeanne's foot down on the accelerator, but she lifted it quickly. She couldn't be doing with being pulled over for speeding.

"Yeah, Jessica," he said. "She was three months when I left."

"How old is she now?" A question designed to see how long he'd been on the streets, whether his absence would be noticed if he had family in the area. And what of that family? Why hadn't be gone to live with them?

"Seven."

"And you've been homeless all that time?"

"Nah, I shacked up with the bird I got up the duff for a bit, but she lost the baby, blamed it on me, then *she* kicked me out an' all."

"Oh dear . . . No family?"

"None I want anything to do with."

"I'll look after you," she lied. "You'll have a lovely room, and I'll feed you."

"Cheers. I can't get over this. Talk about landing on my feet." He rubbed his hands again.

"I'll wash your clothes, too."

"Blimey, who knew nuns were so kind."

It's stitched into them, you prat. It's what they do, being kind. "What's your name?"

"Caleb Pirtle."

"Well, I'm Sister Leeanne."

"Nice name."

She pelted up the nunnery drive, parking behind the house, then took him inside, holding back her irritation at him saying how warm it was, how he hadn't spent time in an actual house in what felt like forever. It was his own stupid fault, the situation he was in. How could he not know that?

If you'd kept your dick in your pants, you wouldn't be a filth. You'd be at home with Jessica, watching her grow up.

"I'll show you to the bathroom. There's a dressing gown in there you can use while your clothes are in the wash. The other nuns are out at church, so don't worry about having to explain who you are."

After she'd settled him up there, she went to the kitchen to make the fry-up he'd requested — "Can't beat a plate of bacon and eggs, innit!" — and boiled the kettle. The magic potion she needed to send him to sleep sat in a bottle behind the coffee canister, all ready for use.

It was going to be a good evening, she just knew it. Another Dillon captured and, come tomorrow, he wouldn't exist.

CHAPTER SIX

Bethany and Mike stood at the warehouse door, Mike pointing his torch beam on it, at chest level. He knocked, and a three-inch gap appeared, a beady eye in a weather-beaten face peering out, white hair a coil on a shoulder.

"Who's there?" Curmudgeon asked, gripping the edge of the door with a gnarly set of fingers, the knuckles swollen and red.

I should have bought him some gloves.

With the darkness behind them and the light facing him, he probably couldn't see who they were.

"Hi, it's Bethany Smith. We met outside the café earlier."

He opened the door wider and stepped outside. "Ah, come to turf us out of here, have you?"

"No," she said. "I'm here with Mike, my colleague, to ask about Karl."

"Aww, got himself into trouble, has he? That's not like him."

"Can you tell me a bit about him?"

"What do you want to know for?" He eyed her with suspicion.

Should she tell him now? Rip the plaster off and be done with it? "I'm sorry to have to say this, but his body was found this afternoon."

His face crumpled, and he staggered a step backwards, bumping into the warehouse wall. "Oh. Shit. Did the cold get to him? I wondered where he was lately. He's always here with me or at the shelter come the nighttime."

"No, it appears he committed suicide. Do you think that's something he would do?"

"Karl? No! He has a head on his shoulders. Likes the nomadic life. All right, he loved being able to get clean and eat, don't we all, but other than that, he was happy enough. Better a life out here than at home, that's what he said. His mother . . . I heard a lot about her from him. A rum sort. All about herself and the gin."

So that's what was in her glass. "I see. Did he mention a father at all?"

Curmudgeon shook his head. "Never knew him. All he had was her, and he left when he was a lad. I would have done an' all. I met him a month after he arrived here, and no matter what I said, that kid wasn't going home. Some do, once they know about the pitfalls of street life. I tell them a thing or two, and it sends most scuttling back to their mums."

"Apart from the man who stole something from Karl's bag, do you know of anyone who would want to hurt him?"

"Hurt him? Well, yeah, there's plenty who would hurt the likes of us. Some spit on us as they go past, and we might get just a kick if we're lucky, but others, they'll beat the shit out of you given half the chance. We're scum to them."

Bethany's guts rolled over. She'd been living under a fucking rock and was ashamed of herself. "If this place" — she gestured to the warehouse — "were to become operational, would you consider working for the shelter?"

"What, with proper pay? What do I need money for? They already feed me, let me sleep here. What more do I need?"

Could life really be boiled down to only needing food and a place to lay your head? Curmudgeon had deliberately shunned what society said you needed: The latest phone, the car, the house, the brand-name clothing, the hairstyle, the position in the class system . . . It was endless, these material things, but what you really needed was love, to feel secure, and a bit of dinner in your belly. Nothing else mattered, did it?

She smiled, belatedly realising he couldn't see it. "It's just that I've put things in motion, and the money might come in to get the beds the warehouse needs. Are you willing to talk to the press, to help get the word out?"

He nodded. "If it means people get to kip in a bed and not on the floor, yep. You just tell me when." He smiled back, nodding as if to confirm it to himself.

"A lady will come here, tomorrow night. Her name's Angela Hill, okay? She's with the paper."

"Fine, but she'd better be on the level. I don't want no pious bugger interviewing me. I chose this life, it didn't choose me."

"No, no, she's lovely. I'll let her know you'll be here, all right?"

She asked to speak to everyone inside the warehouse and addressed the collective, a raggedy bunch, too thin, faces speaking of hunger and strife, despair. No one had seen Karl for a long time; they'd assumed he'd found a new evening spot for begging and somewhere else to lay his head. Of course, no one knew where that was.

They left them to it then, Bethany never so glad she'd bought Curmudgeon that sleeping bag. It was extremely cold, and her nose and fingertips were numb as they walked to the main shelter. Sandy let them in and said they could speak to the people in the dormitory, and again, she did it as a collective, many of them too tired to be hanging about waiting to be spoken to individually. They must have walked around all day, maybe taking a breather on a public bench or rooting in bins for food.

No one had seen Karl or knew of anyone who would hurt him.

Frustrated, Bethany dropped Mike at his place, then went on to hers. She had a shower, then put on her fleece pyjamas, mindful that so many didn't have that luxury. Guilt poked her as she got into bed, with its thick quilt and clean sheets, her radiators on low to keep her warm throughout the night.

She wanted to fix the whole world, but a section of Shadwell's residents would have to do. If she could get that warehouse up and running, she'd at least done something. She remembered what she'd said to Curmudgeon and quickly messaged Angela at *The Herald*.

> Bethany: CURMUDGEON WILL SPEAK TO YOU TOMORROW NIGHT AT THE WAREHOUSE BEHIND THE SHELTER.
>
> Angela: EXCELLENT. THANK YOU!

Mind swirling with not only what had happened today but the plight of the homeless, it took Bethany far too long to fall asleep.

CHAPTER SEVEN

Caleb was still coming to terms with where he was. A room with gruesome pictures on the walls, so horrible his legs had gone to jelly. And those legs, his body — he couldn't move, couldn't get himself off the thing between his legs.

A leather strap, like a belt, held him to something behind, and going by the shape of it on his back, it was a pole of some sort. He'd find out if that was true if he could turn his head, but the damn thing wouldn't shift.

And, God, he had no clothes on. Bruises covered him, as though he'd been beaten up while he'd slept. His muscles ached, everything so sore. What had happened? Where had he been before this? Had he not made it to the warehouse?

Mind sluggish, he tried to remember. Something about a woman in black seemed familiar . . . and getting in her car. Ah . . . she'd driven him somewhere, and on the way, he'd told her about Jessica and what he'd done behind his ex's back. The woman had shown him sympathy, as if what his ex had said about him wasn't true, and that maybe he wasn't a lying, cheating bastard who didn't deserve to be loved and trusted. Didn't deserve a beautiful daughter. It'd been one night, one mistake with her best friend. A drunken decision that had brought him to this, homeless and God knew where.

Click.

What was that? His heart rate tripled, and he strained his head to twist it, but for fuck's sake, it wasn't complying. He needed the loo — damned if he was pissing here — and struggled to hold it inside. His bladder, so distended, hurt.

Another *click*, then a shuffle or two.

"You're awake, filth."

He jumped, letting out a pathetic squeal, and pushed himself to move, to get away. The voice, he knew it, had heard it before. Did it belong to the woman in black?

A fucking nun, that was it. He'd come to her place, had a shower, and she'd fed him a fry-up, the best thing he'd eaten in years. And the tea, two cups, one normal, the other strange, bitter, and he'd asked her if it was Earl Grey or one of those weird, newfangled efforts. Chai. He'd heard that tasted odd until you got used to it. One of the people at the shelter had said about it; someone had bought him one when he'd sat outside Costa in the hope of getting lucky.

"What . . . where am I?"

"You're in your room, you twat. Where else did you think you'd be?" she said, out of sight. "I told you I'd bring you here. Don't you remember?"

Yeah, he remembered now, her promise of a bed for the night, and clean clothes. She'd lied, the bitch, and when he got off this bloody pole, he'd give her what for. If he had to hit her to get away, then that was what he'd do. He didn't hold with doing that and had been brought up never to raise a hand to a woman, but this was all kinds of fucked up, and it was a case of survival, self-defence.

She appeared, sudden and frightening, in front of him. Her face . . . White with black circles round her eyes. What the hell was that all about? Her lips, they were black, too, like she was some kind of demented ghost. The white nightie added to the illusion, and he instinctively made to rear back, going nowhere, his body still not listening.

She jabbed her fingers to the sides of her head and did this strange thing, moving her hands. Mad, that was what she looked like. Some crazy cow, nothing like the nun he'd gone with, but it was her, he was sure of it. Where were the others? Had they come back from church yet? She'd said that was where they'd gone.

"Hungry?" she asked. "Yes, you must be hungry. It's been hours since you last ate, and a homeless belly is a bottomless one. At least you don't stink now."

No, he didn't stink, but his skin was a mess, what with the bruises. "What happened to me?"

She lowered her hands and put them behind her back. "I beat the shit out of you for what you did to me. You're an arsehole, Dillon."

Dillon? What was she going on about? "I'm Caleb. I don't know any Dillon. You've got me mixed up with someone else." Relief zipped through him. That was what had happened. She thought he was another man, and if he could make her see he wasn't this Dillon bloke, everything would be all right.

"You're *all* Dillon, every single one of you lot." She walked behind him, and something rattled.

He shifted his eyes, a trolley coming into view. Despite his predicament, his stomach rumbled. There had to be food under that silver dome, and yes, she was right, he was hungry. He always was these days.

She parked it in front of him and picked up a fork, waving it about. "You'll eat everything I feed you. It's mushy, so you won't have to chew. Good job, really, when you can't use your teeth. I suspect you can't move much at the moment."

She giggled.

He was dribbling — why hadn't he noticed that before? He tried to swallow the spittle, relieved when his throat worked. He blinked and wondered if she'd drugged him with something that immobilised him. It must be wearing off — he was able to twitch his fingers. *Why* drug him, though? What had this Dillon fella done to her that she had to resort to this?

"Can you . . . can you get me down so I can eat?" he asked.

"Oh, no need for that. I already said I'll feed you. Don't you *listen*?" She hissed that last word at him, her breath fanning his face. "Meat is what you're having. Muscles, fat, like I had to have. Raw — everything about that meat was raw. Everything about that *sausage*." She paused. "Don't tell me what to do, Stout Farmer."

Eh?

He shuddered at how vacant she appeared, maybe lost in the past, or inside her bizarre mind. And she *was* bizarre. Her eyes . . . was she watching something playing out in front of her, something only she could see? She'd bent her head, fork poised by her face, the tines glinting from the light above, a bare bulb hanging from a short flex.

"You shouldn't have done what you did to me, Dillon." She snapped her face up to stare at him. Reached out without breaking eye contact to lift the dome. Put it on her head.

He blinked a few times, trying to get to grips with what she'd done, then had to look away — her inspection of him was too much, too intense, like she wanted to peer right into his soul, see his secrets, his needs and wants. He swerved his attention to what was on the plate. She hadn't been kidding. Raw meat, mushed up as if she'd run it through a blender on the 'chop' mode, not puree. White bits dotted it, jagged chunks of what must be fat.

He couldn't eat it.

"Don't even think about it," she said. "And I know you are. No muffins available. You need to eat what I ate. Need to know what it feels like. Payback is a bitch, you filth, you bastard."

A thought crawled into his mind then, of his ex, Michele. Had she set this up? Had her hate for him festered over the years until she couldn't stand it anymore and had planned this . . . this torture? He managed to shake his head. No, she wouldn't have resorted to this. Keeping him away from Jessica was punishment enough. Sometimes, he'd walked to his kid's school, watched her in the playground, the struts of the iron fence railings getting in the way until he pressed his face between two of them, gripping them hard. He'd been chivvied away on several occasions, with threats of the police being called, and he'd told the teacher who he was, that he just wanted to see his little girl, but she'd told him to move on or else.

He'd missed so much by thinking with his dick.

Sister Leeanne — was she really a nun? — scooped up some of the meat and came closer.

"If you don't eat this, I'll force you to." She smiled sadly. "Actually, I want to force you, so it's the same as me *back then*, taking something against your will."

Should he do what she wanted and refuse? Would it work out better for him if she got what she needed, some kind of closure to do with a bloke he had no clue about?

He clamped his lips shut and would do whatever it took to make her get lost.

"You fucker," she snarled, whipping her hand up, pinching his chin between finger and thumb, forcing his mouth open. "That's it, Candy Girl, take it all," she said in a man's voice. "Take everything I've got."

Candy Girl? Oh God, this was awful. What the hell had happened to her?

The cold wetness of the meat settled on his tongue, and he gagged at the taste. Blood. He swallowed without chewing, retching all the while, the damn stuff passing down his throat only to come back up time and again. He steeled himself to get it down him, to make it stay down, and swallowed. She shovelled fork after fork in, until no more could fit, the damn stuff oozing out, dripping over his chin.

"Full, so full," she said, man-voice. "You can't take anymore, but I'm still going to carry on. You love a bit of Dillon, don't you."

He thought about what she'd said, about the sausage, and his mind went to a place overflowing with darkness and debauchery, where this woman had endured something she never should have, if he'd put two and two together right.

Christ . . .

With the plate empty, she stepped back.

"You'll be sick after all that. I was. Nearly every time." She took the dome off her head and rested it over the plate. Dropped the fork onto the trolley. "I waited until you were gone, Dillon, so you wouldn't know. Held it in." She walked backwards, to the far wall, and licked the image of a man. "*This* Dillon is gone." She sniffed the picture. "Just like you will be."

She pressed a small button, one he wouldn't have seen otherwise, lost as it was amongst the depraved drawings.

"You will kill yourself," her voice said, but her lips didn't move.

How had she done that?

He glanced about, his head moving at last, panicked in case another woman was here, one of the nuns she'd mentioned. Were they all just as twisted as her?

"You will use the weapon," crackled out of somewhere.

She withdrew something from a pocket in the nightie and approached. It was then he spotted a wooden pole beside him, and she placed the item on top.

A candy cane?

"You will stab it into your stomach."

His arsehole spasmed, and he fought desperately to keep himself from defecating. She stepped back and wheeled the trolley behind him.

"You will obey."

"You will be no more."

"Kill yourself to make everything better."

"For you . . ." A freakish pause. "For me . . ."

A rattle of the trolley wheels.

A click.

Silence.

"You will kill yourself . . ."

The voice repeated what it'd said before, over and over, and he closed his eyes, stomach churning. Everything he'd eaten came up, and, just like she'd said, he was sick.

* * *

Leeanne watched him from the computer in her bedroom, pleased to see that disgusting meat on the slate tiles. Dillon had got what he deserved, but it wasn't over yet. She'd karate the fuck out of him again in a bit, so he could feel it this time, every kick, every punch. He'd know then, what it was like to be in pain.

Caleb-Dillon had regained the use of his arms and legs and pathetically tried to get the strap off his torso. It was tight, so it dug into him, and the pole between his legs . . . she hoped it hurt, like a certain other 'pole' had done to her.

Dillon had a lot to answer for. Look how screwed-up she was. Look how broken.

Bastard.

She got on her bed and closed her eyes to the tinny sound of her recorded voice chanting at him. She'd set her alarm for three a.m., and in no time, it woke her. Energised, she went to The Room, circling him, his snarling demands to be set free telling her he hadn't reached the pitiful stage yet.

That would come. Soon.

Leaving her voice playing, she mimed the words and walked to the back, to the picture of the other Dillon. She tasted him, shoving her breath out so he'd know what that felt like, how disgusting it was, then ran at this new Dillon, full pelt. She kicked him, a roundhouse to his head, which snapped to one side, him shouting out that she was fucking mental, you nutty slapper, and I'll kill you if you don't pack it in.

She ignored him, kicking, chopping, punching until he was a limp mess, hanging there from that pole. Her adrenaline rush waned and, out of breath, she stood a few feet from him, miming, "You will stab it into your stomach."

He lifted his head, wincing, his stupid face puffy, lips split, eyes blacker than the original Dillon's heart, and stared at the cane on the pole.

"Do it," she said between her voice's orders. "Put yourself out of this misery."

He reached out, hand shaking, and grasped the cane. Probably thought if he gripped it, he could use it on her if she came close. He held it in front of him, the pointed end aimed at his stomach, and she sucked in a breath, waiting for him to cut himself.

They glared at each other for long moments, her exhaling, him snorting, his nose broken, off to one side, blood still dripping from it.

"Do it," she said.

"You will kill yourself," her voice said.

"No." He shook his head. "No fucking way."

She moved forward and then kicked his wrist, sending the cane into his guts. He gawped down at it, at his hand still holding the curved end, then pulled it out.

Blood spewed.

"More," she demanded.

He hovered it over the wound. "No. Please, no."

She ran behind him, reached round, and gripped his wrist. Stabbed him while he grappled with his free hand to stop her. Her strength beat his weak limbs, and after several deep stabs, she let him go. The cane sailed to the floor, landing in the meat sick. *She* hadn't killed him, *he'd* done it. His hand had wielded the weapon, not hers.

Back in front of him, she watched, fascinated, as blood gushed out, onto his groin, his legs, dripping on the floor. One trail slithered down his big toe, plop, plop, plopping into a crimson puddle.

"I hate you, Dillon." She reversed to press the button on the wall, and her voice stopped chanting.

He peered at her through those swollen eyes of his, and if hatred were a tangible thing coming out of them, it would wrap around her neck and choke her now. His head dipped, leant to one side, and his breathing grew shallow. There it was, that rasping, the death rattle.

Silence.

The air so still.

Job done.

* * *

Come seven a.m., a river of blood on the floor, the meat an island, Leeanne uncoiled the water hose from the wall beside the door and jetted the mess away. It slithered down the slight slope in the corner and into a hole, where it went directly into the sewer. Such peculiar things were discovered in old houses. Why that hole was there, she didn't know, and Maggie hadn't either. Sometimes, rats made it up the pipe, and she killed them by whacking at them with a shovel.

She showered him with water, the gadget on the end of the hose creating a jet-wash effect, his skin rippling from the pressure, his wounds filling, the water opening them right up, several gaping mouths.

Leeanne got to work drying Dillon then wrapping clingfilm time and again around his belly, then up to his armpits and down to his groin. She duct-taped it so no blood could escape; she didn't need it dribbling here, there, and everywhere.

By eight, gloves on, she'd loaded him into the passenger seat and strapped him in with the clingfilm-covered seat belt. He was a blob of purple and black, his mouth hanging open in a grotesque shape, his clothes in a pile on the square of plastic on the back seat. She'd written the note and placed it in a sandwich bag, and now it was time to make the delivery.

She'd chosen the cemetery before as a gift to Maggie, who rested there, round the corner of the church at the back. She hadn't wanted to risk dragging him all that way, so the tomb at the front had served a purpose. This time, she'd pick another place, one for Mother, to show her, like she'd done with Maggie, that bad things happen when you don't properly look after the child in your care. That child turned bad and sought revenge.

Maggie had put her in danger, Mother had been oblivious.

These other Dillons had to pay.

In her habit, sunglasses in place, her mouth covered by *his* black-and-beige-striped scarf, she drove away, into the city, to the nearest supermarket. Round the back in the delivery bay entrance, she parked, the place silent. She'd half expected the metal roller door to be open and had anticipated the thrill of dumping him in plain sight. With no excitement on that score, she got him out and sat him against the front of a wheelie bin, the place of Leeanne's birth. Leaving a little something with him, she sped off, thinking of the CCTV and how the police would be chasing their tails over her false number plate.

Life was fun sometimes.

Back home, she drew the latest Dillon on the wall in The Room, with that cane jutting out of his belly, his mouth the same as it'd been in the car. God, she felt good, ridding the world of filth.

Her next job was cleaning the cane, and then sleeping. She had to get a few hours in before tonight, when she started all over again.

CHAPTER EIGHT

Bethany had not long stepped into the incident room when a call came in from Rob at the front desk. Another naked body, this time behind one of the supermarkets. She instructed Fran and Leona to delve into the long list of names Sandy had given her for the homeless — the poor sods would be at it all day — and left.

The drive to the crime scene took five minutes, and she parked at the edge of the delivery bay behind a SOCO van. The photographer did his thing amongst the rust-coloured slush still lingering from where grit hadn't quite got rid of the snow, and other officers were in the process of getting a tent out of the van. Isabelle stood yapping to a colleague, so Bethany and Mike headed towards Tammy, who held the log.

"Morning," Bethany said. "What a start to your day."

Tammy grimaced. "Not what I thought I'd be doing when eating my breakfast. I envisaged a nice, quiet shift."

"That's a joke around here." Mike signed in then wandered off to get protective clothing from the van.

Bethany scribbled her name and the time. "Did Kribbs speak to you yet?"

Tammy's eyes widened, as though the thought of the chief talking to her scared her shitless. "No . . ."

"Want me to give you a heads-up?"

Tammy nodded. "Please."

Mike arrived with the gear, so Bethany got dressed.

"You're on my team after Christmas."

Tammy widened her eyes. "What? I'm allowed to go for my DC exam?"

"Looks like it." Bethany smiled. "I need you with us. We're so busy all the bloody time. An extra pair of hands will help massively."

"God, wait until I tell Charlie." She laughed. "I'm well excited."

"You'll smash it. Anyway, back to work . . . Who found the body?"

"One of the employees pushed the roll door up ready to take some packing cardboard out to the wheelie bin. She found him there at about eight-twenty."

"Okay, we'll go and see her now."

"It's Dawn Mercer. She's gone to the staffroom."

"Thanks." Bethany waved and walked away, calling to Isabelle, "Be with you in a bit."

She went inside with Mike, strolling up to a security guard positioned in front of a door at the back of an area stacked with cans on pallets encased in transparent plastic. Holding up her ID, she told him who they were and asked where the staffroom was.

He gave them the once-over, as though their protective clothing brought home what was going on. "Er, through this door, down the corridor and it's the room at the end."

They followed his directions and entered. A woman sat at one of the many tables, another lady beside her.

"Dawn Mercer?" Bethany asked.

The one with red eyes and pale cheeks held up a hand, then dropped it to the table. "Yes?"

"Hi, I'm DI Bethany Smith and this is DS Mike Wilkins. We're here to talk about the discovery you made." She pulled a chair from another table and sat in front of Dawn. "Can you go from before you opened the roll door, please?"

Dawn picked up a scrunched tissue and ripped a strip off, her hands shaking. "I was going out to put some cardboard in the wheelie bin — I'd been flattening boxes since about seven this morning. I had a bloody great pile, so it took me a few trips to leave it on the ground and then go back for more. I'd just got it all in the bin — I'd stood to the side of it — when a leg and foot caught my eye at the front. God . . ." She sniffed and pressed the tissue to her nose. "It was awful, like it wasn't really happening. I stood there, staring, and thought: That's never a leg and a foot, is it? There were bruises, so many of them, all over." She shivered. "I didn't know what to do, so just stood there for a second. Then I walked round, slowly, and . . . and it was a body. It had clingfilm or something around the middle, and tape on it. More bruises. I moved to stand in front of him — I saw *it*, you know, between his legs, so knew it was a bloke — and his face . . . Shit, I'll never forget it. Someone had beaten him up, and his nose looked broken."

This brought back memories of Karl, and Bethany cursed the fact that a killer had decided to fuck Christmas up for so many people.

"Did you see anything else?"

"Clothes, and a piece of paper in a bag. And he had a carrier on his head."

What? "Okay . . . What sort? One from this shop?"

Dawn nodded. "Yes."

"What about before work? Where do you park?"

"You know just as you turn into the delivery bay? There's a car park the staff use. I left my car there and came into the shop from the front."

"What time was that?"

"Six-thirty. I start at seven but like a coffee before I get going."

"Right. Were there any deliveries before you went out there?"

"No, the first one's due at nine."

Great. They'd have to send him away to deliver at the main doors instead when he turned up. "Who else was in at that time?"

The other woman spoke up. "Just me at six. I'm the manager, Su Biela. The other staff who were in about six-fifteen didn't come out here — they walked to work and entered through the front before going straight to shelf-stacking. Only two of them. They didn't leave the shop — I already checked the CCTV. However, the camera did catch the body being left there." Su closed her eyes for a moment. "I watched it . . ."

We have a sighting of the killer? Brilliant. "What about other staff? This shop opens at eight, so . . ."

"We have three on the tills that early," Su said. "They all get the bus in, and again, they came in through the front at seven-thirty. They dropped their bags off in here and went straight to the tills."

So no one had seen anything out the back. Thank goodness for cameras.

"We'll need to view the footage," Bethany said.

"You can come to my office." Su rose and placed a hand on Dawn's shoulder. "I think you should go home."

Dawn nodded, sniffing.

Mike took her address and phone number, and she left the room. Bethany and Mike followed Su down the corridor and into her office, where she sat at her desk and wiggled the mouse to bring her monitor to life. On it was a still image, the camera pointing from above the roll door. The view was of the delivery bay. A foot was just visible behind the farthest wheelie bin of a row of six, all of them standing side-on against a wall.

"I'll rewind it to where the car came," Su said, clicking her mouse.

She did that then pressed PLAY. The time stated just after eight and ticked along a few minutes in semi-fast-forward. A dark car arrived, parking with the passenger side facing the bay. Someone got out and rounded the vehicle, opening the door.

"Is that a nun?" Mike asked.

Bethany squinted. It appeared so. Black dress, headgear, and a white band across the forehead. The face, though, was obscured with sunglasses and a scarf, one end of which flapped in the cold breeze over her shoulders.

Was this a woman — or a man dressed like one?

She hauled the body out, carrying it like a baby in both arms — she had to have strength to do that, so they were looking at someone who possibly worked out. The nun walked across the bay and placed the body down, then returned to the car, closing the passenger door and opening the one at the back. She reached in, brought something out, and disappeared behind the bin. It resembled a pile of clothes.

Christ Almighty . . .

Then she got back in the car and drove away. It had all taken three minutes.

"Can you rewind it a sec so we can zoom in on that number plate, please?" Bethany asked.

Su did that, but with the image blown up so much, the plate was fuzzy, impossible to make out individual numbers and letters.

"I'll need this footage," Bethany said.

"Shall I give you the one outside the front as well?"

"Please."

While Su sorted that out, collecting a data stick from a drawer, Bethany got her chatting about the homeless of Shadwell and whether she'd be interested in taking in donations from shoppers.

"We have some charity money boxes we could use," Su said, transferring the data. "I could ask all those working the tills to encourage people to put money in over the next few days, if you like."

"That would be brilliant, especially with people possibly feeling benevolent over the Christmas period. If you could take the money round to the shelter at, say, the end of business on Christmas Eve . . . I'll let the lady there know you'll be coming. Her name's Sandy Cossar."

"That's fine, I know her. I'm allowed to take food there at the end of each day. It's all the stuff that will spoil quickly and that we didn't sell at a reduced price. The cook there works wonders with it, especially using the veg for soup."

"That's brilliant. We're trying to get the warehouse up and running to help more people get a bed for the night."

Su handed over the data. "I hope the donation drive works."

Bethany pocketed the stick and left Su to it, walking down the corridor with Mike. They entered the delivery room and then went out into the bay. The tent was up, and Presley's car sat behind Bethany's.

Inside, she held her breath, dreading looking at the body. If it was as bad as Dawn had said, it wouldn't be pleasant viewing.

"And how are you two today?" Isabelle trilled.

"Fine until the call came in," Bethany said. "I was hoping Karl was a one-off, so we'd actually get a Christmas where we weren't working. Now there's a second one, we're looking at coming in over the break if we don't sort it quick."

"That's the shittiest bit about our line of work," Isabelle said. "I'm meant to be going to my sister's. Fat chance of that."

"Maybe we can get this wrapped up and leave the paperwork until Boxing Day," Mike said. "Surely even a killer has to maintain appearances and be at home over the holiday. If she has family—"

"Wait, *she*?" Isabelle's eyes bugged over her face mask.

"CCTV picked up a nun," Bethany said. "It could be a man, but if it is, they're slender."

"Bloody hell." Isabelle shrugged. "When I think nothing can surprise me anymore, something does. To carry bodies, she has to be fit. Strong."

"She cradled him like a baby," Mike said, staring at the body. "Oh, he's in a bit of a state . . ."

Bethany had been avoiding looking, but she'd better get on with it. They had to take the data stick to Fran and

Leona, then, if there was a note left behind again, visit the next of kin. She shifted her eyes in his direction, and he was as Dawn had described. Someone had indeed beaten him up, just like Karl, and the number of bruises showed just how much anger that person had. What had these men done to her, for God's sake?

A pile of folded clothes sat on a plastic square, as did a note, again in a sandwich bag.

CALEB PIRTLE. THIRTY-ONE. HOMELESS FILTH.

So, this woman, if it *was* a bloody woman, had a problem with homeless people. Why? Had she been homeless herself and came into contact with them at some point before she'd pulled herself out of that life? Whatever, this was another brutal attack, one which didn't appear to be suicide this time.

Why had she covered the belly up? The clingfilm was smeared pink beneath the many layers, so blood was present. Had she gutted him?

"Is it possible to cut that film off him in situ?" she asked.

Isabelle said, "In this instance, we need to know what's going on with his belly, so yep, let's cut that film, at least just the middle bit." She turned to the photographer, who was in the corner snapping images of another bin. "Can you get a record of us doing this, please," she said. She knelt and used a scalpel Presley handed to her. "Actually, you do it, Pres. I don't want to further damage anything underneath."

While they swapped positions and Presley painstakingly slit one layer after another, Isabelle nattered on about station gossip, leaving Bethany wondering how she missed it flying around. Mind you, she didn't like to stand at the proverbial water cooler and dig for dirt, but this slice of information might affect her.

"So, apparently, Kribbs is going to be looking into recycling some employees, sending them elsewhere." Isabelle narrowed her eyes.

"He hasn't said a word to me about it. In fact, he's agreed to Tammy Hill joining my team while she does her DC training. That's a good couple of years, so I'd say we're safe. You work hand in hand with us, so you lot should be okay, too."

"I thought the same, but I'll keep my ear to the ground, and see if I find out anything else." Isabelle sighed. "I'm buggered if I'm moving on again. I've settled in well here."

"I'd hate to see you go. Anyway, it's just rumours. Let's not face it unless we have to." The news had unsettled Bethany. Everyone rubbed along fine, so the idea of changes brought on a touch of anxiety. She wished Isabelle had kept it to her bloody self.

"Okay, here we go," Presley said.

Bethany looked at Caleb. *God . . .*

"Multiple stab wounds to the stomach," Presley said, "and what's interesting is that the skin is sliced, but the wound inside is like a cylinder."

"What do you mean?" Mike asked.

"Think of something with a blade on the end of a tube," Presley said.

"That's just weird." Isabelle frowned.

"The tube is about a centimetre wide, but long." Presley peered at Caleb's stomach, shining a torch on it. "That goes back quite a way. Perhaps six inches. There's one particularly violent stab, as if the blade/cylinder was pushed in with great force, but the others aren't so messy. This is going to sound unbelievable, but going by the angle of the others, it appears he stabbed himself. That first one, though, had pressure from the front, so he might have punched the hand holding the weapon."

"Eh?" Bethany frowned right along with Isabelle. "Or someone did the big stab, then he finished it off?"

"I'll know more during the PM, but it seems so." Presley inserted the temperature instrument. Waited. It beeped, and he read the little window on the side, head cocked where he worked out the time of death. "Between three and five a.m."

"What I don't get is," Mike said, "if he was killed at that time, why risk dropping him off when they could be seen doing it? Why not bring him out here straight after when everyone's in bed?"

"For the thrill?" Isabelle suggested.

"Or they want to get caught," Bethany said. "But really, who *wants* that? Unless, of course, they know what they're doing is wrong and can't help themselves, at the same time hoping to get nabbed so they don't do it again." She shook her head. "I know we have to try to see things from the killer's point of view in order to apprehend them, but honestly, I really hate doing it." She gave Caleb one last glance. "And what the hell is that carrier bag on his head all about?" It had been put there like a hat, the handles resting beside his ears.

"No bloody idea," Isabelle said. "We don't half get some whacky cases."

"You're telling me. Right, we have to go. I need to get Fran and Leona on this CCTV footage, plus checking the roads leading to here to see if we can spot the direction that car went. Then there's the nun angle. Do we even have a nunnery or whatever around here?"

"Don't know," Mike said. "Come on, let's get going."

They signed out with Tammy, took off the protectives, then left, the trip to the station a little longer than the one to the supermarket, what with traffic thicker due to people going to work. It was creepy when you thought about it. All those civilians minding their own business, looking forward to the festive break, when just a short way from them, a body sat propped against a bin, never to see another Christmas again.

CHAPTER NINE

In the incident room, Bethany told Fran and Leona the latest.

"Did you find anything out while we were gone?"

Fran clicked to a window on her monitor. "I've made a start on the names of the homeless. About seventy aren't even from around here. They've landed on our patch for whatever reason — debt, drugs, eviction, marriage breakups . . . I've spoken to a fair few family members already. None of them have priors before they got here, but some have been warned about begging, a couple of them brought in for repeating the act after being cautioned not to. Just another hundred or so to get through . . ."

Leona piped up. "I've looked at CCTV on roads heading towards the church, and only three were in the vicinity at that time of the morning — one black car, two light ones. ANPR picked up the plates. Two exist, one doesn't. The legitimate ones . . . I phoned the owners, and they were on their way to work. The cameras don't go right up to the church, but the turning those people took leads into the city. The unidentified one carried on, obviously going to the church."

"Okay, that makes sense. The car used to deliver today's body is dark." Bethany moved to the kettle to make them all a coffee.

"I've already done the CCTV around the supermarket," Leona said. "No sugar in mine, ta." She pointed at the cups. "I'm trying to cut back so I can binge on goodies at Christmas and not put any extra weight on."

Bethany laughed. "So you're losing weight first, then when you put it back on, you'll be the same as you were before? I like the way you think."

Leona smiled. "I'm a genius. Anyway, back to this CCTV. It stops just before the main turning into the supermarket. At six, a car went to the supermarket, which belongs to a Su Biela, then another arrived at around six-thirty, which belongs to a Dawn Mercer. Around six-fifteen, a couple of people walked that way, and at seven-twenty-five, three got off a bus then walked."

"They're fine, they all work there. We've spoken to Su and Dawn." Bethany spooned coffee granules into the cups.

"Okay, so at eightish, can't remember the exact time, a dark car heads there, looks like two people in the front. It returns three and a half minutes later, just the driver."

"So you got a good look at the occupants?" Bethany poured boiled water.

"Luckily, yes, if a bit grainy. Now this is where it gets odd." Leona tapped her pen on her desk.

"I think I know what you're going to say, but carry on." Milk added, Bethany stirred the drinks.

"Ugh, spoiling my big reveal," Leona said. "The driver appears to be a nun, going by the headgear, and wears a scarf over her mouth, but the sunglasses . . . a lot of the snow has gone, so you can't tell me the glare is that bright to need them, and it's murky out today, so there's no sun. Now, the passenger appears to be male with a busted-up face, head lolling. From what I could see, he's naked, but there's a strip of something or other going across his chest beneath his armpits." Leona grimaced. "I have to say, since working on this team and dealing with weird things, it did cross my mind that the passenger had their breasts removed."

Bethany handed Fran and Leona their drinks. "Not quite. The strip is duct tape, and it was holding down clingfilm that had been wrapped around the torso to hide stab wounds."

"Oh, lovely," Fran said, taking her cup. "Thanks."

"What for, the coffee or the visual?" Bethany smiled.

"The coffee, woman." Fran blew then took a sip.

"Cheers." Leona put her cup on a coaster. "So we have a killer then and not another suicide?"

"Whether it's a killer or not, we're after someone dumping dead bodies," Mike said. "Caleb was stabbed with a distinct weapon — a blade on the end of a cylindrical handle, so perhaps a craft knife? Presley said one of the wounds was inflicted from the front, force used, but the others, the victim likely did it." He took his coffee from Bethany. "I'd love to know how he can tell something like that just by looking."

"Years of experience." Bethany thought back to the past. "Do you remember that Kathy, the last ME? I wonder if she'd have picked up on that so fast."

Mike shuddered. "I didn't like her, such a know-it-all. I was glad when she moved on. Didn't she go where Tracy Collier is?"

"Yeah," Fran said. "Got married and went to help Gilbert — he's my dad's mate. He's been thinking of retiring for a while but never seems to get around to it. That's why Kathy went, to take over from him, but they've just carried on together."

"Well, that's all very interesting, but we've got shit to do," Bethany said. "I know I changed the subject in the first place, so count that as me also telling myself off for it. We have two homeless people, both suspected suicides, but what if they aren't? Someone knows they're dead, otherwise they wouldn't be dumping the bodies. Did you run a check on Caleb while we were gone?"

Fran nodded. "He's lived here all his life. Doesn't speak to his brother, the only living relative apart from his daughter, Jessica, who's seven. Her mother is a Michele Turner, who's happy to speak to you today. Although, note I haven't told her what's happened yet. She assumed that he's in trouble again. His brother, Steven, is currently serving overseas, actually *in* the sea. Navy. Submarine. He'll need to be informed; I didn't want to do that without your say-so."

"Yep, get on to the relevant people and ask them to pass that along." Bethany glugged some coffee. "Any priors for Caleb?"

Fran lifted her cup. "A bit of a prat as far as I can see. Cautions going back to his teenage years — stealing, vandalism, causing a nuisance — then he moved on to bigger things: ABH, GBH, he was put away for the latter. Two months. Had a punch-up outside a pub and glassed some bloke. After that, it went quiet . . . ish. Parking fines, a disagreement with a neighbour. Then Michele kicked him out — I'll let her tell you that particular story — and he went to live with another woman. She kicked him out as well, and he was homeless from then on, so the last six years."

"Sounds like he was a right bugger," Bethany said.

"His parents died when he was sixteen. His brother, older than him, took him in for a couple of years, then Steven joined the navy to make something of his life. Maybe Caleb was a mess from losing his family and ended up in trouble."

"If his brother is on submarines, makes sense why he didn't go and live there after the women got rid of him," Mike said. "Shall we go and see what that's all about?"

Bethany nodded.

"Keep your eyebrows down," Fran said. "Because you'll want to raise them well high when you hear what Caleb did."

"You teasing sod." Bethany smiled. "I could make you tell me, you know."

"Yeah, but where's the fun in that?" Fran swivelled to face her monitor.

Before they left, Bethany decided to go and see Kribbs on the pretence of filling him in on what was happening. She actually wanted to see if the gossip Isabelle had told her was based on reality or just rumours. She made him a quick coffee, taking hers, too, and then walked down the hallway. His door was open, and he glanced up at her standing in the frame.

"Ooh, that for me?" he asked. "Come on in."

Fuck me, he's in a good mood. She stepped inside and lightly kicked the door shut, then sat opposite, handing him his drink. "Just nipped in to give you the latest."

He sighed. "Not before Christmas, surely . . ."

"Afraid so. Two bodies, one yesterday, the other this morning. Only just got the chance to tell you." To nudge him in the direction of the gossip, she said, "So I'm glad Tammy's joining the team. We can't carry on as a four for much longer. Fran and Leona are always run ragged."

"Hmm, yes, wise move having her aboard. I'll be talking to her later to let her know. Impeccable worksheet, that one. Good choice on your part."

"I thought so." It was obvious he wasn't biting, so she might as well just ask. "Tongues are wagging, by the way."

He lifted one eyebrow. "About what?"

"The words used were 'recycling employees'."

"Ah. Chinese whispers, eh? Well, between you and me, the only recycling I'm doing is sending Tammy your way and letting you have Glen Underby on major cases. Some people do love to bandy things about, don't they. I've noticed that although you and your current team work absolute wonders, it isn't fair, when the big jobs come along, that you've got to run yourselves into the ground. Are you happy to have Glen to hand?"

"Definitely. He's a brilliant copper." She slumped in relief. "I must admit, the gossip had me worried."

"Unless you hear it directly from the horse's mouth . . . Speaking of horses — or mares — my ex-wife's attempt at getting my money got thrown out of court."

Shit, she hated it when he confided in her like this. "Oh right . . ."

"She got greedy. I already give her a grand a month, and she wanted more. Where that was supposed to come from after my living expenses I don't know, but she had it in mind to take half of my private pension, something she never contributed to. As you know from our last little chat, we had separate bank accounts and put equal shares into the bill pot." He sipped and swallowed.

"Glad you got that sorted, sir."

"Oh, I did, and I have another little snippet for you."

Please don't . . . "What's that then?"

"There's romance on the horizon."

The image of Kribbs getting amorous with a woman popped into her head. *Bloody hell . . .* "Lovely."

"One of the cleaners here, would you believe."

"That's great, happy for you. Sorry to cut you short, but I have to get on. I just need to quickly fill you in and then I have to visit someone." She babbled the case details before he could stop her, then got up and left.

In the hallway, she blew out a long breath. Why had Kribbs decided she was his sounding board since his wife had ditched him? He'd never confided in her before that. Perhaps if he started seeing the cleaner, he'd tell *her* his secrets instead.

She grabbed Mike and drove them to Michele Turner's, a nice little semi in the better part of the city. They gathered in the kitchen, leaving Jessica, a pretty little thing, watching *The Grinch* in the living room, laughing her head off. Michele offered tea, but they declined.

"So, what can you tell us about Caleb?" Bethany asked, the dining chair hard and uncomfortable beneath her backside.

Mike, next to her, appeared to be having the same problem. His grimace said it all. Pen poised over his notebook, he bent his head.

"He's a useless cockwomble," Michele said.

That was a new one on Bethany. "And that means?"

"A twat." Michele sighed. "I look back now and wonder why I ever got involved with him. Maybe it was his bad-boy image, his confidence, I don't know, but he's never grown up. He's stuck being twenty, still speaks like he's that age, innit this, innit that."

Nice . . . "When was the last time you saw him?"

"When Jess was small, when he cheated on me."

Oh. So that's what Fran was on about. "I'm sorry to hear that."

"I'm not — not anymore. I'm glad he did it. Means he's not in our lives."

"So you kicked him out?"

"Yes, from my old house. I swapped with another council tenant and came here, so he didn't know where we were. He kept coming round to the other place, see, being a pest and shouting outside the window at night, that sort of thing. He'd moved in with the woman he'd cheated on me with — my best friend, by the way, best friend no more. He got her pregnant, she lost the baby, then she turfed him out an' all. Apparently, he was homeless after that. Slept on a few people's sofas at first, one night here and there, until they got sick of him."

"So you haven't seen him since then?"

"No, but people talk and tell me things, even though I ask them not to. I don't want anything to do with him, and I certainly don't want Jess exposed to someone who's been in trouble with the police. Like I said, when you look back, you wonder what on earth you were doing. I was young — that's my excuse."

"These people who tell you things. What do they say?"

"Oh, just that they saw him begging outside one shop or another, and he's filthy, thin. I should feel bad for him, I know, but what he did to me . . . Sorry, no sympathy here."

I wouldn't have any either. "It's a shame you went through that. Are you okay now?"

"Yes, just me and my Jess. Don't need anyone else."

"Okay, this question might sound odd, but what were you doing last night and early this morning?"

Michele frowned. "We went to the cinema, then had dinner at Pizza Express. This morning . . . we haven't been out yet. I was going to drop Jess off at Mum's so I could nip to Argos and get a few more stocking fillers, but your workmate said you'd be round, so I stayed put."

"Have you seen anyone today?"

"Yeah, my next-door neighbour popped here about eight for some milk. Why?"

"Do you know a Karl Hartley?"

Michele shook her head. "Should I?"

"Probably not." Bethany took a deep breath. "Do you see Caleb as the type to harm himself?"

"If you're talking emotionally, yes. Look what he did to me and Jess, and really, by doing that, he hurt himself. If you mean physically, no, he hasn't got the balls. He's a coward."

"Do you know of anyone who would want to hurt him?"

"Apart from me, you mean? No. And I wouldn't actually hurt him, by the way."

"I realise that. I don't like being the bearer of bad news, but Caleb's body was found this morning."

Michele's faint smile from her last comment faded, and her cheeks whitened. "Um, pardon?"

"He was found behind a supermarket. He'd been stabbed."

Michele slapped a hand to her chest. "Bloody hell . . . I don't know how I'm supposed to feel about that."

"Do you think he would stab himself?" That sounded so ludicrous, given that they had a suspect, but with Presley's view that both men had probably committed suicide, she had to ask.

"Absolutely not. I told you, he hasn't got the balls, unless life really did a number on him and he didn't think it was worth carrying on. I can't see that myself. He's been on the streets for years. Why kill himself now? You'd think he would have done that years ago when everything kicked off and was raw." She paused. "Unless it all got bottled up, and he couldn't stand the mess he's made of his life. Did you get hold of his brother, Steven?"

"Someone is doing that today."

"They don't get along. Steven is a completely different person. He actually pays me child support because Caleb doesn't bother."

Wow. "That's incredibly kind of him."

"It helps a lot. I only have a part-time job during school terms so I can be off on the breaks with Jess. Without his money, I'd sink, to be honest."

Bethany got up. "We'll leave you to it. Again, sorry to deliver that news right on top of Christmas."

Michele smiled sadly. "I suppose I'll have to tell Jess, even though she doesn't know him."

Mike rose. With nothing to say to that, they said goodbye then walked to the car and got in.

"That's one decent human being," Mike said. "Steven, I mean."

"I thought the same. I suppose it's back to the station then, to look into nunneries, but first, I want to swing by the café in case Curmudgeon is there. Maybe he knows Caleb and can shed some light on this shit fest."

She drove there, but the old man wasn't around. They'd have to work a bit later and visit him at the warehouse. Bethany detoured to the shelter and spoke to Sandy Cossar again, who had a similar story to tell about Caleb as Michele had. A loser. Arrogant. Someone the others steered clear of.

"So, yes," Sandy said, "he could well have a few enemies."

The question was, which enemy tied the two men together? And why?

CHAPTER TEN

Leeanne couldn't get the wire to twist together. Maggie had given her an old coat hanger, the metal sort, and she was supposed to create a circle so she could help make a Christmas wreath for the front door.

Maggie had set up a table in the middle of the U-shaped seating in the caravan. They sat opposite each other, Maggie sorting the plastic holly leaves and berries, plus the mistletoe to put on the 'masterpiece' Leeanne would create. There were also pretty gold balls, and they had thin, bendy wires that would be easier to attach.

"It hurts my fingers," Leeanne said. "Can you do it?"

Maggie took the coat hanger and, quick as a wink, formed a circle. "There. Now you can add all the lovely things." She'd attached wire to the leaves and handed a bunch over. "Just put them next to each other all the way around. It'll be so bushy."

Leeanne gave it a go, getting pricked by the holly for her trouble. "Ouch!" She pushed on, pleased at how it was looking once she'd got the hang of it.

"Dillon will be staying with us for Christmas," Maggie said. "Won't that be nice?"

Leeanne's tummy rolled over. No, it wouldn't be nice, it'd be horrible.

"He's going to stay here, in the caravan," Maggie went on. "I don't want him sleeping in the house anymore. Do you know why I don't want that?"

Leeanne shook her head.

"Because Dillon needs to understand you must be left alone in your room."

Did Maggie know Dillon visited? She must do if she'd said that. But if she knew, what would Dillon do to her?

"I don't want him in there either." Leeanne attached a golden ball in amongst a cluster of red berries.

"Why's that?"

Leeanne shrugged. She couldn't say. Dillon had told her that Mother and Maggie would get hurt if she did. Then he'd kill her. While she didn't care about Mother, she loved Maggie and wouldn't want her in any pain.

"Do you need to talk to me about anything?" Maggie pressed.

"No. I'm okay." Leeanne didn't want to think about him. "Tell me why Mother put me in a carrier bag."

She'd heard the story so many times before and had never understood it. Maggie always said it was all Mother could think of doing so no one would see her with a baby. She'd hidden her pregnancy, letting people assume she'd just got fat, and when it had come time to have Leeanne, she'd hidden behind a wheelie bin round the back of the supermarket, in the dark, alone.

"Your mother had heard about me from one friend she'd confided in," Maggie said, the tale told exactly as it had been before. "So, once she was able to walk after she'd had you, she put you in the bag and came here."

Once, Maggie had mentioned a cord that goes between a woman and a baby, and Mother had cut it with some sharp scissors she'd taken with her and used three wooden clothes pegs to clamp the end closed.

"Your mother is so brave." Maggie sighed. "I'm not sure I could have endured the same all by myself. She's blessed to have you."

Mother didn't act blessed. She was nasty, a mean old bag.

The wreath was complete, and Maggie played Christmas tunes on her harmonica for a while, Leeanne singing along, then they left the caravan to hang the wreath on the nunnery front door. They stepped back on the drive to admire it, and the crunch of gravel behind had them both turning, Leeanne hiding in Maggie's skirt, trembling.

"Ah, Dillon. You're early," Maggie said, resting a hand on Leeanne's head.

"Thought I'd come and help put up the tree." He smiled, his broken front tooth revolting. One corner had chipped off. His stupid hat was like a dome, covered in patterned material that Maggie said was from the army. A camouflage helmet or something like that. He'd been a soldier once. "I was also thinking we could make paper chains."

"That's very nice of you," Maggie said, "but you're not due until tomorrow, and I promised Leeanne we would do the tree on our own."

Dillon sniffed. Rubbed his thingy like he did in her room. "But it's cold out."

Maggie released a breath. "I know, but someone else is staying tonight."

Dillon kicked at the gravel then stomped off down the drive.

"Who's coming tonight?" Leeanne asked once he'd gone, gazing up at Maggie.

"No one, child."

"But you said . . ."

"I know, I know. I lied, and that's very naughty. I won't do it again."

But Maggie lied again that Christmas. Leeanne counted every one.

* * *

Dillon loomed over her. He must have left the caravan and crept into the house. How did he get in, though? Maggie always locked the doors before bed. A cold breeze wafted in. Had he climbed through the window?

"I've got a present for you," he said. "Taste it."

He shoved what felt like a straw in her mouth. Toothpaste-flavoured, all minty. Sweet.

A candy cane.

"Now taste this one."

The sausage.

CHAPTER ELEVEN

Bethany sat at the spare desk in the incident room and browsed local nunneries while everyone else got on with the other jobs. The only one in Shadwell had closed years ago after the last nun, Maggie James, had renounced her faith and bought it. There had been a piece in the paper about it, and some people had been reported as annoyed that she'd turned her back on God. Still, the place had to be checked out — Bethany had done an information search on the property, and Maggie had signed it over to a Zoe Paling a while before she'd died. Zoe was also deceased. It now belonged to a Leeanne Paling.

"We need to go out on a visit," she called over to Mike, then got up to write the name and address on one of the whiteboards. "See if the resident knows if there are any other nuns about."

She drove them there, chatting until they arrived — about the state of the roads now the snow had turned to slush, but how it would soon be a white layer again, according to the weather bloke. Or how high they had to have their heating lately, and how black ice was lethal.

Lingering snow was banked up at the sides of the gravel driveway, but the centre of it was clear apart from a smattering of mini white hills that had an icy crust. The grey house bricks were aged and large, and an ornate stone arch curved over the wooden front door, creating a small, open porch. A holly wreath with mistletoe and golden balls hung from the knocker, a bright-red ribbon at the top, tied in a bow. It was all very festive, like something on a Christmas card. The place could be mistaken for a manse.

She parked in front of the garage to the right, and they stood on the front step after pressing the bell. It took a while, and another press or two, then a woman answered. She could be death warmed over: pale face, black rings around her eyes, dark lips, blonde hair a right state, dry and brittle. Was she ill? Her appearance and nightie suggested that much, although it was odd seeing a young woman in a granny's clothing.

"Leeanne Paling?" Bethany took her ID out and held it up. "I'm DI Bethany Smith, and this is DS Mike Wilkins. We just need a quick word if that's okay." She wasn't sure if she wanted to catch whatever lurgy this woman had.

Leeanne stared. "I'm not properly awake, but come in. I've been asleep."

They stepped into a large foyer with a pew to one side and the floor flagstone, giving the surroundings a cold, churchy air. Bethany shivered, and Leeanne closed the door. She raised both hands, fingers pointing, as though about to press them to her temples, but she lowered them to her sides instead.

She must have a migraine or something.

She led them to a kitchen, where a real fire burned behind a mesh guard. Everything was so *old*, as though it hadn't been changed for a century, the porcelain sink deep, like in a farmhouse, the cupboards wooden and in good need of sanding down and revarnishing. At the kettle, the only modern thing around, she shifted a small glass bottle out of the way containing clear liquid, then set the water to boil by prodding the switch a bit too hard.

"D'you want one?" she asked, turning only her head to peer at them over her shoulder.

Cripes, she's one scary-looking bugger. "Not for me, thanks."

Mike said the same.

"We won't be long. I can see you're not well." Bethany smiled.

"What kind of unwell do you mean?" Leeanne faced away again, her voice monotone. "Not right in the noggin department?"

Eh? "Um, no. Do you have the flu or something?"

"Yes, that's it. The flu." Her shoulders shook.

A weird sensation flickered up Bethany's spine. She wanted to get out of here as soon as possible so intended to press on quickly. *Some people give me the creeps.* "We need to pick your brains about—"

"If you pick them, they won't work right, that's what Maggie said." Again with the shoulders.

Okay . . . Bethany glanced at Mike: *Sort her out for me, will you?*

"Do you know of any nuns around here since Maggie James died?" he asked.

"She was the last one living at this house." Leeanne swung round and leant against the worktop. "She opened this place and had a few living with her for a while, ancient ones, but they died before we got here."

"We?" Mike raised his eyebrows.

"Me and Zoe. I mean, my mother. Maggie used to help people a lot, and she let us live with her after I was born. I was illegitimate and hauled around in a plastic carrier bag."

Dear God . . .

Mike gaped, then snapped his mouth shut.

"We became a family." Her eyelids twitched — the hint of a lie? "Maggie was more like a mum to me than my own."

Mike frowned. "So just to confirm, you don't know any other nuns?"

Leeanne shook her head and then twisted to make her coffee. Her hand strayed to the bottle. "Are you *sure* you don't want one?" Her shoulders shook again.

Is she bloody laughing?

"No, cheers," Mike said.

"Damn." She grabbed the kettle.

Damn? Does she want our company? Is she lonely? On a whim, Bethany said, "Are there any nun's habits still around? In the loft or whatever?"

"I packed Maggie's and Mother's things and stored them. Took their clothes to the chazza."

"Chazza?"

"Charity shop. The Salvation Army one."

"Were there any habits?"

"Can't remember."

"Okay, well, we'll be going." Bethany stood, a bit abrupt, but ho hum. While this woman was acting oddly, she'd rather not be around her. Maybe she'd overdone it on Night Nurse or whatever and wasn't at her best. There were times when she got a strange vibe from someone, and this was one of them. "Hope you get better soon."

She rushed out and, in the car, with Mike sitting beside her staring at the garage door in apparent shock, she said, "Just me?"

"Nope, she was eerie. Eccentric might be the word."

"High on meds, d'you think?"

"Probably, and maybe other drugs we haven't got time to deal with. She looked like shit, didn't she. Heroin, I'd say, going by the shadows round her eyes."

"Hmm." Bethany reversed down the drive. "So if the nuns are dead and gone, we'll need to poke into where you can buy habits around here. Probably in a dressing-up shop or on Amazon. Also ring the branch of the Sally Army to see if any habits were donated. They'd remember something like that — it'd stand out in their minds. Message Fran about that for me, will you?"

"Okay, but we ought to get some lunch," he said, getting his phone out.

Bethany agreed and took them to the café they'd been to yesterday. She parked and was pleased to see Curmudgeon sat outside on a bench, all bundled up in his jacket, with his new holdall beside him. She waved at him as they approached, and his face lit up in recognition.

"How are you today?" she asked.

"Same as every other." He showed his stubby teeth in the semblance of a smile. "Alive."

"I'm glad we bumped into you. There's been a development that I hope you can help us with."

"What's that then?"

"Do you know Caleb Pirtle?"

He nodded. "Bit of a lad, but he doesn't mean any harm, although from what he tells me, he's been in trouble with you lot a few times in his younger years. Why, what's he done, robbed something? Punched someone?"

"There's no easy way to put this. He's dead, I'm afraid," Bethany said.

Curmudgeon shook his head, eyes wide. "Blimey. What's going on around here lately? How . . . ?"

"It's looking like suicide again, but we're leaning more towards murder, so please be careful when you're out and about."

"Looking like? Either he killed himself or he didn't," the old man grumbled.

"It's not as simple as that, and obviously, I can't go into specifics. Do you know if he had enemies?"

"He's a wally at times, but as far as I've seen, he gets along with everyone. What did he do to himself?"

"It was a stabbing."

"I'm no copper, but it sounds to me like it's connected to Karl. Doesn't take a genius to work that one out." He stroked his beard. "But I'll be careful, always am. Trust no one, me. Best way to be."

"When did you last see him?"

"He prefers the shelter if he can get in, but he stayed at the warehouse three nights ago." He patted his chest over a pocket with a zip at the top. "I keeps a note in my little book of who's there and who isn't."

"Have you seen any nuns on your travels?"

"Hmm." He nodded. "D'you know, now you come to mention it, there has been one walking about, up the high street sometimes, always in the evenings."

Bethany's heart leapt. "About what time?"

"Varies. Six once, seven, half past. She just walks up and down, head bent. Always got a scarf over her mouth. Stands to reason." He shrugged. "It's bloody cold."

Bethany resisted shouting out in excitement. "Thanks for that. Would you like us to bring out some lunch when we're leaving?"

"You'll get me fat." He winked. "But that'd be nice, thank you."

Inside the café, while Mike ordered, Bethany sent a message to Fran.

Bethany: GET CCTV FOR THE HIGH STREET, BETWEEN FIVE-THIRTY AND EIGHT OF AN EVENING. GO BACK A WEEK, BUT LOOK AT THE LAST TWO NIGHTS FIRST.

Fran: OKAY. GOT A BITE?

Bethany: CURMUDGEON HAS SEEN THE NUN.

Fran: BRILLIANT!

Mike left the counter and walked outside with a polystyrene food package, a plastic fork and a to-go cup, steam curling from the little slit in the top. He returned to the till and carried a tray over, placing it on the table.

"What did you get him?" she asked, staring through the window at Curmudgeon tucking in.

"Same as us. Thought you might like something other than a sandwich for a change."

She eyed her plate. Sausage, mash, peas and gravy. Curmudgeon wasn't the only one who could get fat. A coffee with a chocolate-powder holly leaf grabbed her attention, and she picked it up for a warming sip. "I've let Fran know to get the CCTV — for the nun, I mean."

Mike sat. "That's a turn-up, isn't it, him seeing one, although if she's got a scarf over her mouth, like in the footage this morning, we're not going to get much from seeing a nose under a pair of sunglasses."

"He didn't mention them, though, so maybe she doesn't wear them at night."

"What's interesting is having her head bent, like she's purposefully shielding herself from the cameras, yet at the same time, she's possibly on the prowl for homeless people."

"Whoever it is knows what they're doing. Do you think Leeanne Paling told us the truth about not remembering having any habits lying around? It's not something you're likely to forget. She said Maggie was like a mother to her, so when packing up her things, surely the habit would stick out as a memory." Bethany cut the end off a sausage and popped it in her mouth. Cumberland. Lovely.

Mike loaded mash and peas onto his fork. "It's not like we can force her to let us search the place, is it. We have to take her word for it. Maybe she was wrecked by grief at the time and just stuffed the clothes into bags, purposely not looking at them."

Bethany understood that. It had been difficult for her to get rid of Vinny's clothes. At the time, she'd given them away to stop herself from smelling them, but now, she regretted not keeping at least one thing. A jumper. A T-shirt. Although his scent would be long gone, touching what had touched him might bring her some comfort. Too late, though. What was done was done.

"Face it," Mike went on, "the only link she has to this case is the nun's clothing, and if she's ill like I think she is, how would she have the strength to carry bodies?"

"True. I'll just message Fran to do a vehicle check on Leeanne's name anyway." She did that then got on with eating her lunch, worried she'd be sluggish all afternoon, what with the heaviness of the food. The gravy was bloody good, though. Bisto always was.

Just as she swallowed the last forkful of gravy-soaked peas, her phone chimed.

Fran: LEEANNE PALING DOESN'T OWN A VEHICLE. MAGGIE JAMES HAD ONE, THOUGH — A BLACK VECTRA.

Bethany: INTERESTING. OKAY, WE'LL GO BACK AND ASK TO LOOK AT IT.

"Right, off to see the weirdo again," she said to Mike then told him about the car.

"Bloody hell. What excuse are you going to give?"

"I'll tell the truth. Two people have been murdered, and we're checking all dark vehicles." She got up. "We can't ignore this. A nunnery *and* a black car?"

"Yep."

They walked out, Bethany nipping into the shop she'd been in before, buying Curmudgeon a pair of thermal gloves. She gave them to him, and he thanked her, his bottom lip wobbling.

She walked away before he could see hers doing the same thing.

At Leeanne's, she parked outside the front porch this time and rang the bell. The door opened, and Leeanne stood there, still in her nightie, head tilted.

"What?" she slurred.

Has she been on the sauce since we were here last? "Sorry to bother you again," Bethany said, "but we forgot to ask last time . . . Maggie owned a black Vectra. Do you still have it?"

She shook her head.

"Mind if we look in your garage, just to check?"

"You saying I'm lying?" Leeanne raised her pointer fingers, like last time, and held them midair.

"Not at all, but we have to see every dark vehicle. Part of our investigation." Bethany had decided against mentioning the suicides/murders. "It won't take a minute, then I can scrub you off our list."

"What list?"

"Of people who own dark cars."

"You're sodding weird."

I'm weird? Pot and kettle!

"Hang on." Leeanne disappeared inside and then returned with a bunch of keys. "It's the smallest one."

Bethany stayed with Leeanne while Mike went to look. He swung the garage door up, stared in, then pushed it down again, twisting the handle and locking it. On the doorstep, he handed the keys over.

"Can I go back to bed now?" Leeanne scratched her head as if she had nits.

"Yes, thank you for your time." Bethany smiled, the door closing in her face.

She drove away, Mike helping her check the cars parked in the street.

"I take it the Vectra wasn't in the garage," she said.

"No, it had stacks of old stuff in it, like you'd have in a loft. Old furniture, vinyls, that sort of thing. No space for a vehicle whatsoever. Suppose we put it down to a massive coincidence."

"Yep, although we'll bear her in mind, however ridiculous it might seem that she's been dumping bodies."

She continued on to the station and breezed into the incident room. "Anything from the Sally Army?"

"No habits were donated," Leona said.

"What about dressing-up shops?"

"None have been hired for six months." Leona shrugged.

"CCTV?"

"Not through with it yet."

Fucking hell. "Okay, cheers."

She went into her office. Computer booted up, she accessed her emails. Isabelle had sent some files of Karl's crime scene — images to be looked through. She downloaded them. Hundreds of the buggers. After two hours of staring at them all, it was clear nothing had been left behind by the person depositing Karl — unless it was miniscule and invisible to the naked eye.

Back in with her team, she asked, "Any luck with the high street CCTV yet?"

"It's only just arrived," Leona said.

"Okay, send Mike some of the days. We'll get through it quicker that way." Bethany strode over to the sideboard. "I'll make us all a coffee." She did that, handed them out, then sat beside Mike.

"I've got last night's," he said.

Watching the footage was usually mind-numbingly boring, but because they had a specific time frame, adrenaline helped Bethany stay focused.

People milled about on the screen, shopping bags weighing them down. This camera, situated outside The Works, showed no nun, and once the time had gone past eight, she got Mike to check a different one. It pointed at a Vodafone shop. At five-thirty, an employee turned out the lights and left via the front, locking up and drawing down a metal grate. Five minutes later, someone parted from the crowd and huddled in the doorway, lowering to their backside.

"Looks promising," she said. "Male, about Caleb's age." She turned to the whiteboards. Fran or Leona must have printed his picture from one of his arrests, as it was taped up there, his name above it.

By six, the shoppers thinned a bit, maybe only ten on the path at once. Six-fifteen, and the woman they wanted appeared from the right. A habit. Scarf over her mouth.

"There she is, the bitch," Bethany muttered.

The nun walked back and forth past the Vodafone shop four times in the space of fifteen minutes, and on the fifth, at six-thirty, she dropped something. Too hard to make out what it was. She strode away, and the man in the doorway lifted the item, glanced up, and his mouth moved. He rushed to his feet and followed her, then went out of shot.

"Shit, what's the next camera?" Mike asked, accessing the list of files. "Got it." He pressed PLAY and went straight to six-thirty. "She's gone down there, see? A residential street."

"The bloody camera doesn't capture enough," Bethany said.

"That's the last one in this row."

"Keep it playing. We might see a car go along the T-junction."

There it was, a dark vehicle, zooming out of the residential and along past the entrance to the high street, the faint shapes of two people inside.

"If that's her vehicle, did he go with her willingly? I know he walked after her, but did she whack him on the head and force him in the car once they were round the corner?" Bethany said. "Outside the shop, she dropped something, he picked it up. How is she getting them to go with her?"

"Ooh," Leona said. "I've got her on here, too. A few nights ago. A quick glimpse, but it's at the other end of the high street from your shots. The camera points to another T-junction, with only the high street road and part of the T visible. She goes down an alley between shops — going from memory, it leads onto a street. Fifteen minutes later, she emerges with a male. They cross over, him walking slower than her, and that's our lot."

"Let me see that." Bethany got up and went to her.

Mike joined them, and Leona played the footage again.

"Okay, same woman — or if it isn't, same outfit." Bethany scratched her cheek. "Get that still to the tech lads so they can determine heights. Hang on, and we'll send you what we've got, too."

Mike returned to his desk and clicked his mouse a few times. "Sending the stills to you now."

Leona's email alert pinged. "Got them." She pressed FORWARD on Mike's, inputting the techs' addresses, attached her images, and then got on with tapping out a message.

"Right, so we have the nun in the same breathing space as two men." Bethany was elated. "Let's get those images blown up and see if we can recognise either of them, though it's doubtful, because they're already grainy. Leona, ask the techs to try to reduce the fuzz as well, please."

"Will do."

"CC me on that email and ask them to reply to both of us."

Bethany and Mike sat together again at his desk and enlarged the stills. No luck. Neither the nun nor the man from the Vodafone doorway were recognisable. Leona reported the same problem. Bethany's email tone dinged on her phone, and she had a quick look. Presley had written to say he'd be sending a full post-mortem report for Karl soon, but he'd ruled it a suicide.

Fuck. Just what I didn't want to hear.

For the next hour, she went through Karl's crime scene photos again, just to double-check.

Pointless.

There was nothing else for it but to go home, defeated.

CHAPTER TWELVE

Leeanne curled up in the caravan, cuddling Mr Teddy. She'd come out here after the second visit from the police — while they'd been in her house the first time, she'd recognised a manic episode coming on and hoped they hadn't picked up on it. Felicity Gray was fighting for dominance, and Leeanne had internally told her to fuck off. The last thing she needed was for those coppers to think she was nuts — thus, someone to keep an eye on. She'd panicked upon seeing them at the front door, and when they'd come back to ask about the car . . . Shit, she'd almost lost it but tried valiantly to appear calm. When she'd said, "You're weird!", she'd been talking to Felicity. That Smith woman looked like she'd thought Leeanne had meant her. Things were getting dicey.

Thank God she'd taken to parking the Vectra in the back garden the last couple of years after she'd cleared out Maggie's and Mother's things. She'd been so happy after Mother's death, too, and now . . . She had to get all the Dillons. Had to kill them so they'd never come for her like he had.

In a bit, she'd have to wash her makeup off then put the habit on, go and find another filth. She was still tired from the last two nights, though, and, as her eyes threatened to close, she contemplated leaving it, trying again tomorrow evening.

No. No.

She set her phone alarm for an hour's time, thinking it might be a good idea to hang about near the shelter around seven. Those who hadn't secured a place usually loitered, hoping one more would become available for them by some miracle. She knew. She'd watched them countless times, milling about on the pavement, ants around sugar.

Hope, it was a lying bastard.

* * *

Mother sat on the sofa, with a glass of champagne mixed with orange juice clutched in her spindly hand. Leeanne sat in the chair by the door, as far away from her as she could get without being called out on it. Maggie knelt beside the sparkling tree, sorting through presents, ready to distribute them, and Dillon . . .

Dillon stared at Leeanne from the other chair opposite, behind Maggie, and the tree shielded him from Mother being able to see him from the left-hand side of the room.

He rubbed himself. Smiled.

Leeanne's tummy hurt.

"Now then," Maggie said. "Let's open the biggest ones first, shall we?" She passed a large box to Leeanne, wrapped in paper with candy canes all over it.

Dillon laughed at that.

Leeanne shivered.

"Go on then," Maggie said, beaming. "See what Father Christmas brought for you, child."

Leeanne got off the chair and sat on the floor, ensuring her nightie dipped between her legs so Dillon couldn't see anything. The top of the box reached her head. She stripped away the paper to reveal a pink word: BARBIE.

Leeanne smiled. It was on her face before she could stop it.

"Lucky bitch," Mother muttered.

That took the shine off things. Now, Leeanne stopped the emotion showing — Mother would use it against her while they were alone, giving her a slap on her backside for daring to be happy — "Happy, when I had to have you, and I didn't even want you. He forced me, and look what happened, you fucking little wretch!"

Tears filled Leeanne's eyes. Mother would make sure this Barbie and her lovely, three-storey house got 'accidentally' broken. But while she could, today Leeanne would play with it under Maggie's watchful eye.

"I'll help you set it up," Dillon said. "Have you got her a Ken as well, Mags? Barbie needs a man in her life." He laughed again, lurching off the chair to settle beside Leeanne, reaching for the box and opening the flap. "Like you do," he whispered. "A man with a sausage."

Leeanne's face flared with heat, and she folded her lips over her teeth and pressed them together.

"What was that, Dillon?" Maggie asked, glaring at him.

Mother giggled. "Argument incoming!"

"Nothing," Leeanne said.

Maggie didn't seem convinced, but she handed Mother a present, which she tore at rudely. Her smile almost had her looking nice, like she'd never say a bad word to anyone. She clutched the bottle of posh pink gin to her chest. "Cheers, Maggie."

Dillon came next, and he had a black scarf and gloves with beige stripes. "Are you taking the piss or what?" He gawped at Maggie. "She gets gin, and I get these?"

"I thought you'd need them in this weather," the old nun said. "Thought you'd be grateful."

"Well, you can fuck right off." He got up, threw the items down, and stormed out of the house.

"Is he gone for good?" Leeanne asked, struggling to take Barbie out of her box. She was stuck in there with stupid wire on the cardboard backing.

"Yes, love," Maggie said. "I won't allow him to come back again."

Another lie.

* * *

Christmas Day was almost at an end, and her Barbie house sat in the corner of her bedroom, the doll reclining in her bed, just like Leeanne.

A scraping sound, then a muffled curse — "Shit!" — and Dillon appeared on the front porch roof, staring in through the window. She squashed down a screech, her tummy tightening. The soft glow of her lamp on her chest of drawers beneath the window highlighted him. Breath held, heart thundering, she stared at the leering face of her tormentor, his exhalations fogging the glass. He moved his head away and wrote in the condensation: LET ME IN. It was backwards, but she knew what it said.

She shook her head, drawing the cover up her face to just below her eyes, peering over it. He pressed the window, then again, jimmying it, and the stupid loose catch slipped away . . .

Leeanne rushed out of bed and ran towards him. Dillon had opened it wide, his head sticking in, his grin vile, and she reached out and touched his head and pushed and . . .

He fell backwards, crying out. A dull thud filtered up. She moved the lamp across and clambered onto the drawers, leaning over the sill. Beyond the arched ledge of the porch, the top half of his body was just about visible in the gloom. He must have twisted mid-flight, as he'd landed on his front, one of his arms at a strange angle. Light spilt from the front door, and Maggie appeared at his side and hunkered down, turning her head to look up at Leeanne. She waved her hand in a shooing motion, and Leeanne closed the window, drawing the curtains, blocking out the wonderful sight.

She hoped Dillon was dead.

* * *

"He won't come back again, ever," Maggie said the next morning at breakfast.

"Where's he gone?" Leeanne looked across the kitchen table at her.

Maggie smiled sadly. "He's living somewhere else. He promised he'd stay away. Everything will be okay now."

Three days later, while Leeanne reached up to close her bedroom curtains one rainy night, she saw him in his army helmet. Outside. At the end of the drive. Staring up. Arm in a sling.

Lie number three.

* * *

Leeanne had washed her Maggie death-face off in the shower. She put the habit on, and the head thing — she never could remember what it was called — and wrapped the scarf around her neck and mouth. Out in the back garden, she got in the Vectra and reversed down the side of the house and drive, and then out onto the street. She checked for parked vehicles with people inside watching for her, specifically those two coppers, but caught sight of no one.

She drove off, glancing across to make sure her leaflet hadn't fallen off the passenger seat into the footwell. Her mind had cleared, the strange mental lapse from earlier long gone, and she sucked in a breath then blew it out slowly. Undead Maggie was back inside her, the woman who fixed everything and made it all better.

Parking in an alley a few buildings down from the shelter, she peered in the rearview mirror to check if her scarf was high enough over her face. Pleased with her disguise, she got out and, with the leaflet hidden up her black sleeve, she locked the doors and walked into the street.

A few filths dallied, the gross bastards, some near the shelter doors, others farther away, as if they knew deep down there was no chance of an empty bed coming up after the usual allocation time but were still chancing their arm. One of them, closest to her, glanced up at her approach — she observed him with her eyes up, her head bent. A metre or so from him, she drew the leaflet out and passed it to him, hoping the deadbeat twat could even read. He stared at it, squinting, and she headed back towards the alley. If he didn't take the bait, she'd go elsewhere. Filths hung about all over Shadwell. Scummy gits.

She disappeared from the street, holding her breath so any sound of footfalls alerted her that he was coming.

Nothing.

"Ungrateful shit," she muttered.

In the car, verging on a massive strop, she did a three-point turn and zoomed towards the mouth of the alley, her headlights off.

A thud. A jolt. A bloody inconvenience sprawled on her windscreen.

She slammed on the brakes and got out, the interior light giving a small amount of illumination, and marched to the front of the car, well arsey. Someone groaned, and an angry burst of wind came at her, lifting her leaflet from the ground, tossing it about in a mad dance then sticking it to her chest. With a growl, she snatched it off and screwed it up, tucking it in the gap between her neck and the scarf.

"Can you get up?" God, it was painful putting on her nice-person voice. Felicity spoke like that.

"Yeah, I just . . ." A man. Him from the street.

"Let me help you, child." She bent over, grasped material, and hauled him upright, biceps bunching. "I'll get you to a hospital."

She guided him to the car and pressed the top of his head until he sat in the passenger seat. This seriously hadn't gone to plan. Back behind the wheel, she shot out of the alley, almost careening with another vehicle. She gave the driver the middle finger and glared, laughing her head off at the shocked expression on the woman's face, then barrelled on for home, the nunnery — and The Room.

* * *

Angela Hill swerved to avoid the maniac screeching out of the alley. What the hell was wrong with people? She slowed on her approach to the shelter, her legs a tad wobbly from the near miss, her heart going mental. Parking outside, she took a moment to calm down before she interviewed Curmudgeon about the warehouse.

God, the things she put herself through for *The Shadwell Herald*.

* * *

Leeanne giggled inwardly. There he'd been, sitting at her kitchen table, nursing a bumped forehead where it had hit the frame at the top of her windscreen. He'd bounced off, landing on his back, and bumped it again on the hard ground. Now, him strapped to the pole, in the Land of Nod, his head injuries were hidden by bruises from where she'd karate-kicked and chopped him, so angry this time she'd felt like beating him to death. Her hate for Dillon and his sausage had reached a dangerous level.

She wasn't letting him kill himself in the room, though. Wouldn't play the voices. She wasn't in the mood to hang this out over the next few hours. She wanted it to happen quicker.

Instead of doing the usual and leaving him naked, she dressed him in an elf outfit and then grabbed the candy cane. She knelt, lining up the point of the bladed end with his big toenail. The tip just underneath it, she smacked the curved end. The blade drove under the nail and into his actual toe. She shuffled back a couple of steps, cracking up as he roared awake, his scream beautiful, him unable to strike out because of the wonders of the second cup of tea. The cane stuck out of his toe, and she laughed at it, at the blood gushing.

She reached out and yanked it away.

Another gorgeous scream.

She repeated lining up the blade with his other big toe, him staring down, eyes wide, his whimpers pitiful. Blade beneath the nail . . . *whack*.

It took him a while to calm down.

"What the fuck are you doing?" he finally screeched, panting, snot dribbling.

What a snivelling wretch.

"You absolute nutter!" he bawled.

"That was an awful thing to do," Stout Farmer said.

"Be quiet, Dillon, you're boring me." She gazed at blood pissing out of his toes and dripping on the floor. "Pretty patterns."

"What?"

"Never you mind, you nosy git."

He breathed fast, a rabid, angry dog. "What have you done to me?" He stared at the elf costume, frowning. "Why can't I move? Where's the nun gone? Who are you? What have you done to your *face*?"

You should see the state of yours. "I *said*, be quiet . . . Too many questions . . ." Yanking the cane out and ignoring his thunderous shouts of pain, she walked behind him and collected the trolley, placing the cane beside the dome. "Time for some more food." She put her version of the army hat on, imagining it was camouflage, and did what she'd done to the others, forcing him to eat the raw meat.

He gagged, he moaned, but he ate the lot.

Then she kicked the shit out of him some more until he puked and zonked out.

* * *

She parked down the alley near the shelter and, about a hundred metres behind the warehouse, on scrubland, she dumped him on the ground. He woke, mumbling, and it was a shame she couldn't see his face, the state of him. His limbs should be working any second, so she sat him up by lifting him under his armpits to test his ability to remain upright, then went against her better judgment and switched on a small torch, pointing it at him.

He wavered and managed to put both hands out to rest them flat on the frost-bitten grass. "What . . . ? Where . . . ?"

"God, you're such a whinger, Dillon."

"Who's Dillon?"

"Don't pretend you don't know." She smiled at what was coming next. On the ground beside her, weapons waited. "Remember what I did to your toes?"

"Oh God . . ."

"No good talking to Him." She thought about his elf suit, how it was one of those cheap ones that could cause a bit of damage if you weren't careful.

Hahahaha.

She bent down, lifted one of the weapons, and held it out. "Use that on the front hem of your lovely outfit."

"Piss off." He stared at it, eyebrows meeting in the middle.

"Do as I say, or I'll slip my cane blade under your fingernails next."

He took it from her, hand shaking. "Why are you doing this?"

"You know why."

"I don't, I swear."

This pleading lark was getting on her tits. Why couldn't he just kill himself quietly, for Pete's sake, without resorting to childish tactics? Some people . . .

"Do it," she snarled and picked up a small harmonica. "First, put that in your mouth, between your teeth, your lips over the edge. You'll need it to clamp down on."

"You're crazy . . ."

Not half as crazy as you'll be in a minute.

He stuffed it in, and she wanted to laugh so hard at the sight of him. It looked like he had metal teeth.

"Now use that." She gestured at what he held.

He rested his thumb on the appropriate part, a small wheel, and gazed up at her.

"Get on with it!" she seethed.

He dragged his thumb down. A scrape-click. A flame.

"Remember, on the hem," she said.

He closed his eyes, crying, silly sobs coming out of him in the form of a wheezing tune from the harmonica, like he was some pathetic kid who wouldn't take his medicine. Annoyed the music didn't sound the same as when Maggie had played it, she just about stopped herself from kicking him in the nuts.

After what he'd done to her all those years ago, this man should accept this punishment without complaint, yet here he was, blubbing.

She stared, willing him to obey.

He did, and the suit went up immediately — that was what happened with cheap shit from China, mega LOL. Flames devoured his torso, snaking up to his neck, then down his arms. He clamped his teeth automatically on the harmonica, and the tune of death sawed out of it while he fell back, bucking and writhing. If he was sensible, he'd roll, put the flames out, but those flames, they'd crept down his legs, racing towards his bleeding, manky toes.

She switched the torch off and stuck it in her pocket. No need for it now, what with him lit up the way he was, that bloody harmonica still playing. She tried to sing *Silent Night* to the tune, but it wasn't sounding right. Snatching up the next weapon in her gloved hands, she shuddered at the crinkling sound of it meshing with the crackling of the flames, his skin burning, the hairs on it snapping, clicking.

Smells like pork and plastic.

She barked out a quiet laugh, waiting for the flames to go out.

It took about three minutes.

With him motionless, breathing through the harmonica in slow, drawn-out off-notes, she walked to his head and went down on her knees.

His skin smoked.

"I was in a carrier bag once," she said and placed it over his hot head, tying the handles beneath his chin. "Good luck breathing in there."

She turned the torch on.

The bag sucked flat against his face, then billowed out, the music wailing with it.

Repeat.

Repeat.

Repeat.

She turned away and faced the warehouse. Waited for the warped tune to stop. Moved the pile of clothes and the note, putting them beside him.

Then ran to Maggie's car and drove away, snow arriving once again, floating down onto her windscreen.

Another Dillon gone.

Bargain.

CHAPTER THIRTEEN

The phone woke Bethany at five in the bloody morning, for God's sake, and she sat up, groggy, grasping blindly for it in the darkness, slapping her fingertips on the bedside table. She grabbed it and stared at the lit screen. Too bright.

Ursula from the front desk.

Bethany sighed and swiped to answer. "Hi." She leant on her elbow, hair falling over half of her face. Tickling. Annoying.

"Sorry, Beth . . ."

"Don't be silly, can't be helped. What have you got?"

"A body behind the warehouse at the rear of the homeless shelter."

"Oh, sodding hell . . ." She pushed the quilt off and sat up.

"Isabelle is en route."

"Ring Presley for me. I'll deal with Mike. Any ID?"

"No. A Sandy Cossar called it in. Apparently, she was on the night shift at the shelter."

"Yep, I know her. I'll get down there as soon as possible. Ta." She ended the call and rang Mike. "Soz, mate, but there's been another one."

"Christ. Okay, I'll be ready in ten."

"Give me twenty. I'll bring the coffee."

In the shower, she scrubbed herself quickly then got out, chilled by the room's semi-warm temperature. The lowered, overnight heating hadn't done much to combat the nip like it usually did, and she slung on some skinny jeans, a T-shirt, and a heavy jumper. Downstairs, kettle boiling, she pulled the window blind up.

"Fuck."

That explained the temperature. Snow had made an unwelcome return, chunky flakes pelting down, creating a knobbly ledge on the outer sill. It must have been at it for hours, as her back garden was covered, perhaps three inches deep already. It had even landed on each line of her rotary, sitting on top of pegs, looking the same as the ends of cotton buds.

She walked off, disheartened. Head inside the hallway cupboard, she dug out her pale-pink wellies and thought about the white stuff wreaking havoc with any evidence left on the body. It would also bugger up the time of death estimate. She should be used to things rarely going right for them, but just once, it'd be nice if a case was clear-cut and solved without roadblocks messing it all up. Who'd have thought the weather would be the culprit?

Wellies on over thick fluffy socks, coffee made and in to-go cups, she stuffed her phone in her pocket, put on a waterproof jacket, and drove to Mike's. She didn't beep in case she woke his neighbours, but he came out straight away — must have been watching through the window — and sat beside her in a fat puffer coat and woollen beanie, rubbing his hands.

"Talk about annoying that it's snowing again," he said, taking a coffee from the cup holder between their seats. "Cheers for this, as usual."

"Glad to see you dressed appropriately like me. If we're going to be outside for hours, may as well layer up." She gave him the details while driving. "So, what do you make of it then? Another homeless?"

"Got to be, hasn't it?"

"Hmm. Can you ring Leona and get her in early? Leave Fran — she deserves to see that lovely little kid of hers in the mornings. Ask Leona to explain to Fran why we left her sleeping. I want Leona on CCTV outside the shelter and the roads leading to that street."

"Okay." He took a swig of coffee, put the cup between his legs, and did as she'd asked.

By the time he'd finished, she'd stopped outside the shelter behind a patrol car. Glen Underby stood to the left side of the building, police tape attached to a rubbish bin on the shelter wall and a streetlamp on the other side.

"Morning," she said, crunching over the snow to him. "Are you making sure no one goes down the back, or does the log start here?"

"Morning." He smiled, white peppering his shoulders and the peak of his police cap. "Tammy's doing the log farther in. We were first on the scene."

"Okay." She opened a cardboard box inside a black sack and took out some protectives. "You should put one of these suits on, Glen. Saves your uniform from getting soggy. God knows how long you're going to be standing out here." She handed a set to Mike.

"Might well do," Glen said.

"Don't you have a coat in your car?"

He nodded.

"Nip and get it then."

He walked off and then returned, appearing snugger.

"Where's Sandy Cossar?" she asked, pulling the suit legs over her jeans.

"Inside. Her office. I asked her not to say anything to the residents. Didn't want mass panic. Hopefully, they're all still asleep, none the wiser."

"Good. So she was the one who found him?" She stuck her arms in then zipped up, glad of the hood. Her head was already damp.

"No, one of the men from the warehouse had looked out and noticed a shape in the distance."

"What, he could see in the bloody dark?" Mike put gloves on, the edges clamping over the hems of his white suit sleeves.

"He was having a walk. Something woke him up, and he couldn't get back to sleep for a while but ended up drifting back off. He woke again about three hours later and went outside. Used his torch."

"Righty-oh," Mike said.

"Unfortunately, he brushed snow off the shape, hence knowing it was a body." Glen grimaced.

"Wonderful." Bethany continued before her sarcasm soured everyone's mood. "Let Sandy know we'll go and see her in a few."

"Will do."

Leaving Glen to his freezing vigil, they ducked under the tape and trudged down the side of the shelter, bypassing the warehouse and heading farther back, where a SOCO van perched, the tracks from its tyres already being filled in by new snow dancing down. A halogen lit up the scene, the light bouncing off the whiteness, creating a blinding visual. A photographer clicked his camera then walked away — he must have finished cataloguing the body's resting place — and SOCO streamed forward to erect the tent.

While they did that, Bethany stopped to sign the log.

"All right, Miss T?" She smiled at Tammy, who'd sensibly put on a hi-vis jacket and her cap to ward off some of the chill.

"A bit cold," she said, "but I'd rather that than be the poor sod behind me." She took the log from Bethany and handed it to Mike.

"What have you heard so far?" Mike asked.

Tammy related what Glen had said, plus, "Did Glen tell you . . . The noise that woke the warehouse man is a bit weird. He said it sounded like wheezing music, maybe an accordion."

Bethany frowned. "What? That's bloody creepy, especially hearing it in the middle of the night. Did you go over to the body?"

Tammy nodded. "Yes, Glen followed so far but stopped because Sandy Cossar was with him. Didn't think she needed to see it close up. The warehouse man went into the shelter."

Bethany thought of him and Tammy walking across the snow. "Were there any other footprints apart from his when you made your way over there?"

"No. I used my torch. There was one set in, one out beside it. I walked to the left of them."

"So whoever it was who killed them must have done it before the snow started again." She got her phone out and accessed the weather app. "Okay, that was about midnight, so there's been over three hours of snowfall since."

"Our footprints were getting covered over again by the time Isabelle arrived." Tammy's teeth chattered. "It's coming down too bloody fast."

Bethany nodded and peered over at the crime scene, a shaken snow globe without the glass ball, the now-erected tent the focal point, and everything almost silent, sounds deadened by the wintery layer on the ground. "Right, well, we'd better get over there."

She smiled and strode ahead, using the third, trodden-down path Tammy and SOCO had made to keep from disturbing anything else. It brought back memories of Karl Hartley's dump site, and she shivered. Her wellies crumped over the blanket underfoot, Mike's shoes doing the same behind her. At the tent, she slid booties over her wellies and then entered, a smaller halogen standing in the corner, being all important and highlighting the star of the show — a mound with some of the snow wiped off in places. She stared at what it revealed. A carrier bag — again. A finger. A foot, blood staining the white dune flurries, although it hadn't dripped, was maybe transfer from the toe, the yellow nail sitting upright, barely hanging on at the cuticle, the flesh beneath raw and angry-looking.

"What the bloody hell has happened here?" Mike said.

Isabelle turned to them. "'Good morning' is usually the first thing you say to someone, but I'll let you off." She lowered her face mask and grinned. "Isn't that just the grossest sight?" She pointed to the toe. "Can't stand feet. So ugly. Either they stubbed it and the nail lifted up, or someone jammed something beneath it and—"

"That is *not* what I want to entertain," Bethany said, "but the second option appears the most likely. That must have been excruciating." She curled her piggies in sympathy. "God knows what else is beneath that snow."

"Well, we're going to rake it off the body now and put it in plastic boxes in case any evidence is in it, so you'll soon see." Isabelle nodded to a couple of SOCOs, and they got on with it.

It didn't take long for most of it to be removed, revealing something Bethany hadn't been expecting. The photographer came over to take pictures of it.

"He's been *burnt*?" Her stomach cramped, and saliva filled her mouth, the prelude to vomiting. She took a deep breath.

"Hmm." Isabelle moved a step closer. "Whatever he was wearing . . . it's fused to the skin. See the hints of green in with the char?"

"Flammable material," Mike said. "That flesh . . . I don't even want to think about whether they were burned alive."

"Sick, that's what this is." Bethany shook her head. "And if this is one of ours, they were homeless, and it's another supposed suicide . . . Sorry, I'm not swallowing that plate of bollocks. Someone out there knows what's going on. These dead men haven't done this all by themselves."

"Of course they haven't." Isabelle shuffled to the carrier bag, which was clearly hiding a head. "Sorry, Mike, but they were burnt before this was put on — the bag is probably what killed them. Suffocation." She gestured to the neck. "The plastic handles haven't melted." She turned to a nearby SOCO. "Evidence sack. I'm going to take this off. Photographer, get this on record please." She took the sack from the SOCO, plus a sort of craft knife, and cut beside the knot. Drawing the bag back from the face, she then pulled it from under the head. Popped it in the sack.

The photographer took more shots.

"Oh dear." Bethany held back a heave. "He's been beaten like the other two."

His face was one big bruise of varying dark colours. Blood caked his nostrils. The skin around his eyes had puffed up. A split bottom lip. And a harmonica sat between his teeth, probably locked tight in a death clamp. *That* was the noise the man at the warehouse had heard? What the hell was it doing in the victim's mouth?

"Contusion to the forehead," Isabelle said.

"Whacked there to be subdued prior to abduction?" Mike folded his arms. "Just thinking out loud."

"It's quite a wallop. The skin's broken," Bethany said. "And his other toe is in the same state as the first — but where's the nail?"

"Could have fallen off onto the grass and the snow covered it," Isabelle suggested. "If that's the case, we'll find it." She stepped back and stumbled. "Bollocks. There's something under this snow." She grabbed a rake and worked until clothing appeared. She continued until she found a sandwich bag. "Definitely the same person then. Photos again, please," she called out. "And after, can someone bag these togs and the plastic sheet they're on?"

The SOCOs did as she'd asked. Isabelle walked out of the way, standing between Bethany and Mike.

"Let's see what this one says, shall we?" She turned the bag over to show the words on the paper inside.

JOHN HANCOCK. HOMELESS FILTH. LOL.

"This is doing my tree in," Mike said. "She's *laughing*." To Isabelle, "Did you get anything back from forensics on the paper and ink used for the other two?"

She sighed. "If I had, you'd know about it."

"Sorry," he said, "but this is frustrating."

"We're busy at the best of times, but with everyone trying to get caught up because of Christmas . . ." Isabelle sounded weary of the system and how the cogs moved so slowly.

"Again, I apologise." Mike smiled, perhaps as a peace offering. "It isn't like usual, where we can do a press release, then everyone gathers from it that they need to stay inside at night. The homeless have no bloody choice about being outside if they don't get into the shelter or the warehouse. They're such easy pickings that it gets my goat. This cow knows how vulnerable they are."

"It's a horrible situation," Isabelle agreed. "But what can we do? Even if we contact *The Herald* and ask them to run a piece on the deaths, how many homeless will spot a newspaper unless they go past or inside shops? Or have the means to access the internet to read articles? Far too many of them will *still* be vulnerable."

Bethany added her penny's worth. "But we *can* ask Sandy Cossar to pass a message on to all those she comes into contact with over the next few days, or however long it takes us to catch the bastard — bitch, I mean. We should go and talk to Sandy now, and the man from the warehouse. We'll pop back once Presley's arrived."

CHAPTER FOURTEEN

Outside the tent, Bethany patted Mike on the back. "It's getting to me, too."

"I feel so fucking helpless."

"I know, matey."

They trudged to Tammy, snow slapping at Bethany's face, settling on her cheeks and her eyelashes. They signed out of the scene, then walked on to dip beneath the tape. Bethany smiled — Glen had a protective suit on and latex gloves.

"You gave in and took my advice then?" she said.

He looked funny with just his face showing, the elastic of the hood bunched in a tight oval. "I did." He grinned, holding his hands up and wiggling his fingers. "These gloves are bloody brilliant."

"They are indeed. We're just going to see Sandy and that bloke," she said. "Want me to bring a hot drink out when we've finished? I'll get one for the others, too."

He nodded. "Cheers."

She rang the bell beside the shelter door, and, down the corridor, Sandy poked her head out of her office doorway. She hurried towards them, a finger to her lips, probably a warning so they didn't disturb the residents by talking when they went inside. Door open, she ushered them in and pointed to her office. While she locked up, they walked along and entered. Curmudgeon sat on a chair by her desk, his holdall beside him on the floor, a cup of tea or coffee in his cocoon hands.

"Oh . . . hello. It was you who went out there then?" Bethany asked quietly, tugging her suit hood off.

He nodded. "I don't manage deep sleeps. A hazard of living rough. Got to be on your guard."

She imagined living like that, in constant fear, and couldn't comprehend it. These poor sods had it so tough.

Sandy came in and closed the door, then collected two folding chairs from against the wall beside it and opened them out. "There you go. Park your bums. Would you like a coffee?" She indicated the machine on a sideboard to the left.

"That would be lovely," Bethany said. "Thank you."

She sat, as did Mike, and while Sandy gathered cups and poured drinks, Bethany dived straight in, her hands getting sweaty from her gloves.

"Tell me what happened."

"I got woken up by a right weird noise." Curmudgeon sniffed. Rubbed the end of his red nose. "Sounded like bad music. Thought I was bloody dreaming at first, as you do, because it was faint. It went on for a while, me trying to ignore it and get back to sleep. I did eventually, then woke up again because someone else in the warehouse kicked over a can of beer while they were out of it. Bleedin' thing was empty so it clattered. I got up, decided to have a bit of a walk — I do that sometimes, in the middle of the night. There's a sense of stillness you get at that time, can't explain it."

Bethany understood that. She'd sat in the darkness at three in the morning so often after Vinny had died, and it seemed as though she was the only one left in the world until the sound of a distant car collided with the peace and broke the lonely spell.

Sandy handed out the coffees. Thanks given, Curmudgeon carried on.

"So I rolled up me sleeping bag and packed it away — you don't want to be leaving anything, even only for five minutes as someone will take it, quick as a wink — and off I went. Saw it had been bloody snowing again, didn't I. First thing I thinks is how cold it's going to be out on the streets today, then I get me torch out and walk up the back. And there's this lump, and I says to meself: *Why's that snow higher than the rest?* Didn't make sense, so I got level with it and swiped some away . . . Fright of me life, I can tell you."

"It must have been awful. What did you do then?"

"Well, I rushed back here as best I could, the snow being deep and whatnot, rang the bell, and Sandy came running. She called the police, and we waited, then they arrived. Sandy told me to come into the office and wait after the bloke PC talked to me, and she went out with the coppers."

Bethany turned to Sandy, who still stood, whittling her fingers.

"What happened then?" Bethany asked gently so as not to bring more distress to Sandy.

She said the same as Tammy, then, "I've never been so afraid. Hearing about the other two was sad, but to actually be involved in it, for the killer to be so close . . ."

"Did you hear anything?" Bethany asked. "A car perhaps?"

Sandy nodded. "I did, but faint, and didn't take any notice because cars do drive by at night. I feel dreadful now. If I'd gone outside . . ."

"You might have been hurt," Curmudgeon said. "I think you did the right thing."

"You did," Bethany said. "No sense in putting yourself in danger, and you weren't to know the car wasn't just passing. Did Angela Hill from *The Herald* come by?"

Sandy nodded. "Yes. Nice lady. She's so invested in helping us. She spoke to me and Curmudgeon."

"Good." Bethany gulped some coffee.

Mike said, "Hopefully we'll get more funds for the warehouse."

"I'm praying for that," Sandy said. "Oh, I just thought. Angela mentioned having a near miss on the way here. Someone belted out of the alley beside the shelter in their car, almost hitting her."

"That's odd." *Someone checking out the back to see if it was suitable for what they had in mind?* "Did she get a good look at the driver?"

"She said it was only a fleeting glance, but all the same, time seemed to slow, so she was able to make quite a bit out, even though it was dark. A lamppost shone on her." Sandy sat on her desk chair.

"Her?" Bethany's skin pimpled.

"Yes, she said it was a nun, although she had a scarf over her mouth."

Bloody hell . . .

"Not to sound dense," Mike said, "but I take it the woman was wearing a habit for Angela to know this."

"Well, I assume so." Sandy rubbed her temples. "I didn't ask. What she did say was the car was a dark one, and a man was in the passenger seat."

Christ. "Okay, that's been extremely helpful. What time was this?"

"She arrived about half seven." Bethany glanced at Mike: *Pass that on to Leona.*

He took his phone out.

"Did you see anyone around when you walked to the body?" she asked Curmudgeon, despite Tammy mentioning only one set of footprints, plus hers.

"No," he said. "Didn't hear anything either."

"Sandy, do you have CCTV?"

"Only directly outside the front of the shelter."

It was better than nothing.

"Can we watch it from, say, six-thirty?"

"I'll just sort that now." Sandy brought her computer to life and accessed the right file. "They automatically save every twelve hours, so I need to look at yesterday's as it would've stopped recording that day at midnight." She clicked it and then selected the time.

On the screen, people wandered about outside.

"What are they doing?" Bethany asked.

"Waiting in case there's a scuffle inside and a place becomes available," Curmudgeon said. He downed half his drink.

"What does a scuffle have to do with anything?" Bethany frowned.

"People get a bit funny about the beds," Curmudgeon said. "A few have a favourite, and if someone else gets it first, they kick up a stink. It's a bit of the old normality, a bed, comfort, something they see as theirs, an anchor, so to have the same one each time is important. When another bloke takes it . . . Can you see how that would feel?"

Bethany nodded. Someone getting in her bed would really piss her off, but this wasn't the same thing. The beds weren't specifically theirs, but she understood their reasoning. "So what happens if they row about it?"

"There's a strict rule," Sandy said. "Absolutely no fighting, shouting, that kind of thing. If you stay here, you behave. The people outside are hoping there's a fight because anyone arguing is asked to leave, their chance at a bed forfeited for two weeks."

"You'd think," Curmudgeon said, "that the threat of that would deter it, but some people are thick as pig shit."

"Right, so with that explained, how long do they hang about there for?" Bethany asked.

"Probably until around eight." Sandy sighed. "Then I have to move them on. Sadly, I sometimes have to resort to threatening to call the police. I don't like doing that *at all*, but we can't risk them getting into spats out there. We might be classed as the cause and get shut down."

The monitor displayed nothing more than a group of homeless by the doors, shown up by the streetlight Glen had tied the police tape to. There were a few more farther along the pavement, sadly in grey shadow, with features obscured. Then . . .

"Stop!" Bethany said.

Sandy tapped the mouse.

At the top-right of the screen, near the corner of the shelter, a car had turned. Even though it was dark, the vehicle was visible as also being dark.

"Okay, play it again, please."

Sandy did that, and two minutes later, someone walked around the corner, slowly making their way up the street.

In a fucking habit.

Oh my God . . .

The nun handed out what appeared to be a piece of paper, then went off the way she'd come. The man who'd taken it stood there for a few moments, staring at it, then ambled to the corner. He paused, looked back, and disappeared down the side of the shelter.

"What's down there?" Bethany asked, still watching the screen.

"An alley, same as the other side," Sandy said.

"Did you recognise that man?" It was a big ask, but maybe his height, build, or general shape was distinctive to Sandy.

"No," she said.

"It's John Hancock," Curmudgeon said. "I can tell by the shape of his bonce. He's a troublemaker."

"How long has he been homeless, do you know?" Bethany asked.

"New on the scene. About three months," he said.

The car shot out of the alley, drawing Bethany's full attention. Another car appeared, white — Angela Hill's, had to be coming from the top-right of the screen. The dark one swerved, almost smacking into Angela who drove towards the front of the shelter. It zoomed to the bottom of the monitor, while Angela pulled up outside.

"We'll need this footage," Bethany said.

"Okay," Sandy said, "but I don't have anything to put it on."

"Can you stick the file in a zipped folder and email it?"

Sandy frowned. "Won't it be too big?"

"Hmm. Maybe. Ever heard of WeTransfer?"

Sandy shook her head. "You use the computer and sort it."

"Can you show me today's footage first? This person or another may have returned later, although John Hancock didn't come back out of the alley, so I'm assuming he's the passenger in the dark car. If this is who we're looking for, they'll be back to put John behind the warehouse."

"This is a right old saga," Curmudgeon muttered.

"I agree with you there," Mike said.

Sandy selected the file starting at midnight. As suspected, the dark car returned and went back down the alley about two minutes past. It didn't come out again until twenty past, snow now falling. Enough time to set the poor man alight, watch him burn, then suffocate him with the bag.

"That's about when I heard the car." Sandy wiped tears off her cheeks. "When it left."

"Don't," Mike said. "Nothing good will come of you beating yourself up over this, trust me. Let's just say, without me revealing any information, if that's John Hancock out the back, you wouldn't have been able to do a thing for him, all right? Absolutely nothing. If you only heard that car as it was exiting, he was already deceased."

"This is just awful." Sandy sniffled.

"It is," Mike said, "but concentrate on the good you do. Think about how many people this charity drive we're doing is going to reach — people who will donate and help get the warehouse habitable. Make that your focus, not this."

She nodded and clicked about on the computer, saving the footage out from midnight to now, then she renamed it. She got up, and Bethany took her place, putting the files into a zipped folder, opening a browser and inputting WeTransfer, then sent it to herself.

"There, that's done. Is there anything else you can remember that you think might help us?" Bethany stood.

Sandy shook her head. Bethany turned to Curmudgeon. He shrugged.

"Okay, we'll be going now, but can I be cheeky and ask if we can take a tray of hot drinks out to the officers?" Bethany asked.

"That's a lovely idea," Sandy said. "I'll go into the kitchen. The hot water urn is always on. Won't be long."

While she was off doing that, Bethany and Mike chatted to Curmudgeon, asking if he thought John had enemies.

"Probably a few," he said. "Like I said, troublemaker. Pain up the bloody arse, to be honest. He was one of those who got territorial about beds. He'd know full well to hang around for a while to see if anyone got kicked out because it's usually him who is." He still clutched the cup, although it was empty now.

Bethany finished hers and put it on the side. "Want me to make you another one?" she asked him.

"Could do, then I need to get back to the warehouse. I like to keep an eye on those in there. By the way, before I left it to go and do my investigating, I called out and asked if anyone had heard anything. Got no answer, so I reckon the other four were still sparko. Will you need to talk to them?"

"Probably best." She handed him the coffee.

"I'll come with you." He got up, grabbing his holdall. "Sandy won't mind me taking the cup."

The woman herself returned with a large tray full of beige plastic beakers, the kind from vending machines, each full of weak coffee, but the heat in their bellies and on their hands were what the coppers would be after, and beggars couldn't be choosers.

She thanked her, and Mike took the tray once he'd stashed his notepad and pen away. Sandy showed them out. Presley's red car was parked behind Bethany's and, still in their protectives, they walked towards Glen. He took a drink. Bethany and Curmudgeon stopped outside the warehouse, while Mike approached Tammy and then vanished inside the tent to distribute the drinks.

Bethany entered the warehouse with Curmudgeon, who switched his torch on and yelled for everyone to wake up. The startled men sat up quickly, blinking from the sweeping beam of light. Bethany introduced herself and then questioned them, but no one had heard or seen a thing. She hadn't expected them to but had to check just the same.

She left them, going to the tent, and Presley gave a broad estimate for the time of death, but it still fitted with the activity they'd watched on the footage. John Hancock, if indeed it was him, had been killed out here, and now they needed to get back to the station to help Leona with the street CCTV if she hadn't managed to watch it all yet, plus do a search on John and see if he had any relatives who needed a visit.

It was going to be another extremely long day.

CHAPTER FIFTEEN

Dillon climbed onto the porch roof again, staring inside. He opened the window. Maggie hadn't got around to getting someone in to fix it. And, just like that, he was in Leeanne's room, clicking her lamp on and then standing beside her bed, while she looked up at him, fearful of what he might do. She was used to the sausage, his touches, his hot breath, but he may hurt her now. She'd pushed him off the roof. He'd be angry.

"You're a bitch," he whispered. "A fucking little bitch."

She gasped, gripping the covers up to her chin, and went to squeeze her eyes shut so the anger on his face didn't knot up her stomach, but in the end, she continued watching. Waiting. Hoping he'd get it over with quickly and then leave the same way he'd come.

"Just you wait and see what's in store for you." And he left her, disappearing through the doorway.

Where was he off to? Was he planning to steal some of Maggie's things like he'd said he would that time? Leeanne got out of bed, padding after him, the light from her room slanting on the burgundy landing carpet. There he was, a shape down the darker end, outside Mother's door, turning the knob with the hand that wasn't in a cast.

Why was he going in there?

She moved to stand by the jamb. Stared inside. Dillon patted Mother, whispering, telling her to 'wake the fuck up', and he knelt, shoving her now, until she groaned, moaning that she just wanted to stay asleep. Too much of that expensive pink gin after dinner meant she was extra groggy.

"I thought you weren't meant to be coming back," Mother whispered. "Maggie said . . ."

"Fuck Maggie," he snarled, all mean and spiteful. "It's time to do what we planned."

Leeanne's tummy hurt. It always did around those two.

"What, now?" Mother pushed his hand off her and sat up.

"I've got the stuff."

"I told you not to use that. It'll show up in tests if they think it's suspicious."

Tests? And who was 'they'? Confused, Leeanne bit her bottom lip.

"It won't look suspicious," he said. "She's been having problems with her ticker for ages. They'll think it's that. Anyway . . ." He stepped back a bit. "I'll put it in the back of her neck. In her hair. No one will see the hole."

What was he going on about? And why was Mother nice to him? Why wasn't he filth like the other homeless people? She always called them that.

"We're doing it. Now." He yanked Mother up.

"Bloody hell, Dill," Mother said, "do you have to be so rough?"

Leeanne tiptoed back to her room and got in bed, closing her eyes in case they came in to check on her. Footsteps. His breathing.

"Hurry up!" Mother.

Then nothing but them creeping off. She scrambled back out, leaning on her own doorjamb this time. They'd gone into Maggie's room at the end of the landing, the door a right angle to Mother's. Her little lamp was on, the curtains open, and the moon shone through the stained glass window. The old woman was fast asleep, Mother on one side of the bed, Dillon on the other.

Mother wrenched Maggie over onto her front, and the nun's muffled cry had Leeanne wanting to run in there to help, but she was frozen, too scared to move. Dillon took something out of his pocket — a bottle — then something else. Using the fingers of his cast arm, he pulled the plastic cap off. A needle! He positioned it at the back of Maggie's head, Mother pinning Maggie's arms to the mattress. He pushed the end of the tube down and put the bottle on the bedside table.

It seemed ages for Maggie to go still after she'd thrashed, then Mother turned her over, laying her out as though she was asleep, drawing the covers up to her chest.

"Her hands, look at them," Dillon said.

Star shapes.

"What about them?" Mother frowned.

"Authenticity," he said, nodding. "I bet people who have heart attacks get fingers like that. Come on, leave her until the morning."

Leeanne darted back inside her room. In bed, she shook, tears falling.

"Let me out the back way and lock up after me," he said. "I'll hide in the caravan."

Their footsteps clattered down the stairs.

Leeanne waited until Mother had stumbled back up, had got into bed, then she quietly made her way to Maggie. She stood beside her, staring down at the wrinkled skin, the dark shadows beneath her eyes, the white cheeks, and the lips that seemed black for some reason, too dark. Her mouth was open, teeth bared, and Leeanne thought about what Dillon had said. Did that mouth mean authenticity, too?

"Maggie," she whispered. "Maggie, it's me, Leeanne. Wake up."

But Maggie didn't. Leeanne stood there for hours and hours, until morning, desperate for the nun to open her eyes and smile at her like she always did.

As the birds twittered in the garden, Mother came in, stared at Maggie, then at Leeanne. "What are you *doing in here?"*

"Maggie won't wake up."

Mother snatched the bottle from the table and shoved it into her dressing gown pocket. "Of course she bloody won't. She's dead, you stupid cow."

Mother vanished downstairs, then the elderly doctor came, glancing sadly at Leeanne across Maggie's bed. He muttered something about Maggie's heart finally giving up on her, then told Mother he'd arrange for Maggie's body to be removed.

Later, when Mother was dressed and enjoying more pink gin, Leeanne took the bottle out of the dressing gown pocket and hid it in her room. She'd keep it. Give it to Mother one day. She'd just need to find a syringe from somewhere, that was all.

* * *

Dillon visited a lot after Maggie had been taken away, laughing and joking with Mother, saying they could be together now, get married. He went into Leeanne's room once Mother was asleep, her flat-out on more gin bought with the stash of money found in a shoe box under Maggie's bed, him doing what he always did, threatening Leeanne with death if she told anyone what he did to her.

There wasn't a wedding. Dillon lived with them, though, and those few years before he'd mysteriously disappeared had been hell.

Leeanne was older, wiser, and she still had the bottle, although the contents had long since dried up. But there were drugs in the house she could use, create a concoction to do exactly what she needed. Medications Maggie and Mother had been prescribed. She could grind them up, dilute them in water.

She decided she didn't need a syringe.

* * *

"I'm so sorry for your loss," the doctor said, a different one who'd come for Maggie, but one who was aware of Mother's heavy drinking. She'd collapsed once, spending time in hospital with a pickled liver, and that week had been bliss for Leeanne.

Things had gone the same way as they had with Maggie. No questions. No suspicious death to worry about. Mother had simply drunk herself into Hell. The magic potion had been added to the gin.

Where was that bastard Dillon now? Why had he left?

Leeanne took it upon herself to find him out there on the streets of Shadwell one day.

And when she did, she'd kill him, too.

CHAPTER SIXTEEN

John Hancock's father rubbed his face, wiping the tears away. He'd calmed down now after they'd dropped the bombshell but still appeared shaky.

"So sorry to have to push you like this, asking questions, but when did you last see John, Colin?" Bethany asked.

"He left six and a half months ago. Said he'd be better off by himself." He shrugged. "I lost my job, got made redundant, and couldn't afford to keep giving him money — he didn't have a job either — so he got arsey. Always was spoilt." He shook his head. "We had a row the last time I saw him — over a pair of trainers, can you believe. I couldn't fork out for them, so he lost his temper. I also said I couldn't pay his phone contract anymore. He stuffed a few clothes in a rucksack, stormed out, and I haven't seen him since. I thought he'd have kipped on a mate's sofa or something, not on the streets. So he's been sleeping rough?"

They all sat in his living room, the tea Mike had made for John going cold on the coffee table. The parallel with Karl leaving home was sad.

"I'm afraid so. In the shelter sometimes, though. We don't have a formal identification as yet," Bethany said, "but we have reason to believe the body is that of your son, hence us informing you. We'll need you to visit him at some point . . ."

Colin nodded. "Of course. I'm just glad his mum isn't around to see this."

Bethany remained quiet.

"Cancer," Colin said. "Five years ago."

"I'm sorry." *First his wife, now his son? God.* "Do you want me to leave you a card that has contact numbers on it in case you need to speak to someone?"

Colin shook his head. "Nah, I've been through it all when my wife died. I know how to stop myself from getting too maudlin. The councillor taught me a few tricks. Let me just write down his friends' names for you. They might know more than me." He did that and handed the sheet of notepaper over.

"Thank you. Someone will be in touch when you can view the body." Bethany rose. "Again, I'm sorry to have brought you such news."

They left, and in the car, Mike thumped his thigh.

"That was bloody rough," he said.

Bethany drove off, towards the station. "It really got to me when he started sobbing. He couldn't breathe at one point, and then when he fell to his knees . . ."

"Don't. I'll never forget it."

They continued on in silence, Bethany shutting out her own anguish, which had chosen the perfect moment, when she was vulnerable from watching a grown man break down, to sneak in and wring her emotions with grief-weighted hands. She had no time to wallow. They had to get back. Bethany had left Leona to check the CCTV on roads leading to the shelter. Fran would be in by now, so she could look into John's social media from before his phone contract had run out — she couldn't imagine him being able to afford to use an internet café unless he'd been begging, but he might well have borrowed friends' phones or laptops. They also had the list of John's friends to poke into.

In the incident room, Bethany sat beside Mike at his desk, and he got to work running checks on the friends.

There were only three, each of them employed at a pharmaceutical place where orders came in from chemists and they parcelled them up ready for delivery.

"That's handy," she said. "We can speak to them all in one visit." She got up and jotted their names and addresses on a whiteboard. She turned to Leona and Fran. "We're off to speak to these fellas — John Hancock's mates. Did CCTV throw anything up, Leona?"

"All footage is from high above the roads on those tall poles, so the cars look small. Plenty of dark ones, though. Zooming in did sod all except make them fuzzy. And that reminds me. The blown-up ones we sent to the techs . . . Nothing, I'm afraid. The footage was too grainy for them to get a clear shot at the number plate or to know the make of the car, even with that software they have that enhances things."

"Shit. Can't say I'm surprised." Bethany sighed. "Fran, what's John's Facebook looking like?"

"He's not on it, but he is on Instagram. Pictures stopped being put up around the time he walked out of his father's, maybe up to a week after, so the contract must have run out. Those he has got up are self-indulgent tripe." Fran blushed a bit. "Sorry, that was mean of me, but he seemed to be in love with himself."

"Isn't that what Instagram's all about, though? Putting up pictures of yourself and your dinner?" Mike said.

"No idea." Bethany shook her head. "I'm not on it. Seems weird to me, putting image after image up. Sorry, but I have nothing that would interest anyone. I mean, the highlight of my year so far was putting up a rotary line by myself. If I was on Instagram, would that mean I'd have to take a picture of it and gush at how clever I am? Fuck that."

The others laughed.

"So what sort of images did John lean towards?" Bethany asked.

"Selfies at the bathroom mirror, showing off his abs." Fran rolled her eyes. "Pairs of expensive shoes, brand-name clothing — he particularly liked taking pics of the labels. There's a Gucci watch on a hairy wrist an' all."

"Probably all paid for by his dad," Mike muttered.

"He didn't have a watch on at the scene," Bethany said. "Not that I noticed anyway."

"Maybe he sold it to get some cash." Fran shrugged.

"Could well have done. What's interesting, though, is his dad didn't see John as a troublemaker, like Curmudgeon suggested," Bethany said. "He just said he was spoilt."

"Maybe he only turned into a dick after he'd left home," Leona said.

"And maybe the spoilt was knocked out of him by being homeless," Fran added. "Anyway, his friends are also on Insta, but they put up things like football memes, jokes, and the odd pic of their kids."

"So if they have kids," Bethany said, "let's assume they also have girlfriends or wives. John being single and spoilt . . . I wonder how they met, why they're friends. What do they have in common? We'll go and find out now."

Leaving Fran and Leona to it, Bethany drove her and Mike to the pharmaceutical place. Inside, they approached the reception desk, where a forty-something man in a lurid yellow boiler suit lounged on a chair, playing on his phone. He glanced up and stuffed his mobile in his pocket.

"Sorry, I'm just holding the fort while the receptionist has a tinkle," he said.

Too much info, but Bethany smiled anyway. "You might be able to help us." She showed him her ID and introduced them, asking about the three men. "They haven't done anything wrong, by the way."

The lift of his eyebrows, then his scowl had prompted her to say that. The last thing she wanted was for the blokes to get grief when they weren't in the shit.

"I'll page them now." He prodded a button on a microphone. "Phillip, Bobby and Damien to reception, please."

A woman appeared, coming through a doorway to the left, and walked behind the desk. She looked at Bethany and Mike, then at Boiler Suit. "Can I help?"

Boiler Suit leapt up and got out of her way so she could sit. "Police. Nothing to worry about. I just called three of the fellas here."

"Oh . . ." She lowered into her chair. "Okay . . ."

Said three men came through another doorway at the back, all black-haired, all with scowls in place.

Boiler Suit patted one of them on the back. "Let's all go through to the break room."

"Where is that?" Bethany asked. "And I'd prefer it if we spoke to the gentlemen alone."

Boiler Suit, clearly affronted, spluttered, "All right, sod you then." He stomped off from where the men had come in.

"Can you lead the way?" Bethany asked them.

"What's going on?" one asked.

"We'll explain when we have privacy," Bethany said and glanced at the receptionist.

The break room was through the rear door and down a hallway, vending machines at the back, vertical blinds at the open window, swinging from the breeze coming in, though why it was open in this weather . . . All three men stood staring, probably wondering what the bloody hell was going on.

"You're not in trouble," she said. "Let's all have a seat, and I'll explain." With everyone around a large table, she took their names so she knew who was who. "Right, I'm DI Bethany Smith, and this is my partner, DS Mike Wilkins, and we're—"

"The police?" Phillip blurted. "What do you want with us?"

"Let her get a word out," Bobby said. "Fuck me . . ."

Bethany bit back laughter. "We need to ask a few questions about a friend of yours. John Hancock."

"That waste of space?" Damien muttered.

Interesting. "Why do you say that?"

"Look, he left his poor old man in a right state," Damien said. "All over some trainers. Tried to get me to let him stay at mine, but sorry, my missus wasn't having any of it, and neither was I. He's got no job, likes spending money that isn't his, and he ponces about in expensive gear he didn't even pay for. I regret the day I bloody met him."

"And how did you meet him?" Bethany asked.

"These two here." Damien jerked his head at his mates. "They've known him since school."

They discussed that, Bethany gleaning that Phillip and Bobby had only remained friends with John for so long after they'd left school because he'd made a point of bumping into them in various places. The pubs. The nightclub. Once they'd met their wives and had children, contact had tapered off somewhat, and funny enough, Phillip's and Bobby's other halves didn't like John either.

"So did he also ask to stay at yours?" Mike held his pen over his pad.

"Yeah, but we turned him away," Bobby said. "We have no room — only got a two-bed. We have one bedroom, the nippers have the other, and as for him kipping on the sofa . . . Nah, wouldn't have worked."

"And you, Phillip?"

"Same, except we have three bedrooms, but we have my wife's gran with us at the moment while the council sort her flat. It was supposed to only be a fortnight, but eight months later, she's still there. Burst pipes wrecked her place. Not that I mind having her. I love the old gal like she was me own nan."

"So with you three saying no to John, where do you think he would have gone?" Mike asked.

Damien shrugged. "Couldn't give a toss, to be honest. I saw him last month, and what a comedown. He was well filthy, nothing like the rich tosser he liked to make himself out to be."

"There's no one that I know of," Phillip said.

"Me neither." Bobby splayed his hands on the table. "Look, I don't want to be rude, but what's going on?"

"Do you know of anyone who would want to harm John?" Bethany asked.

Damien laughed. The other two shook their heads.

"When was the last time you two saw him?" She stared at Phillip and Bobby.

"Last week," Bobby said. "He came into our local, asking to borrow money. Like Damien said, he was filthy, his clothes were smelly and he needed a ruddy bath."

"Did you give him money?"

"A fiver each." Phillip sighed. "We've got families to feed, and we'd only managed to afford a pint or two because we'd got a performance bonus, otherwise we wouldn't have been in the pub at all."

"Did he tell you anything about what he was up to?"

"Yeah, sleeping in some shelter." Phillip frowned. "I suggested he go and patch things up with his dad, but John didn't like that idea. Said he'd lose face. I said doing that was better than roaming the streets. He reckoned it wasn't."

"Did you notice whether he had a watch on?"

"What, that expensive fucker?" Bobby shook his head. "No, can't say I did."

Bethany made a mental note to check if it had been pawned. It might give them a time frame of when John had got desperate for cash — an indication of whether he'd gone with the nun out of the same desperation. It would also help in finding out whether the nun had stolen it from him and had tried pawning it this morning.

They chatted for a couple more minutes, then it was time to throw the news at them and do a runner. Damien appeared to take it the worst — probably because he'd slagged John off to them and felt bad about it now — but all three kept their composure and didn't cry, although the shock had clearly sent them reeling.

Bethany and Mike gave their condolences and goodbyes, and back at the station, Leona was set on the pawn shop task, phoning them all about Gucci watches. Fran had finished on social media, and with nothing else there to help them, she switched tasks to poke around in John's past to see if anything came up there.

They set off yet again to see Angela Hill at the *Herald* office, picking up a sandwich meal deal and scoffing it on the way.

"So you clearly saw it was a nun driving," Bethany asked Angela, getting as comfy as she could on one of the chairs, the foam padding limp beneath her backside.

"Yes," Angela said. "As I told Sandy, it was weird, but everything slowed. Whoever it was shot out from the side of the shelter, almost whacking into me. I had to swerve to avoid a collision. They sped off, and I stopped at the kerb. It shook me something chronic."

"I bet it did. Was any hair showing? I assume she had the nun headgear on, but was any sticking out from beneath it?"

"No, she'd tucked it all in. All I could see was from above her eyebrows to the top of her nose. She had a scarf on, and it was striped, but I couldn't tell you the exact colours. Dark and light — maybe black and white?"

"So you wouldn't have copped sight of the eye colour either."

"No, sorry. The streetlight shone into her car, but that was orange and always makes things that weird peach, doesn't it."

Bethany nodded. "Did you catch the make of the car?"

"No, and I didn't get the number plate, sorry."

"The passenger. Did you glimpse them?"

"Yes, a man, although it was just the sense of him. I was more focused on the woman and the fact a nun was driving so dangerously — *and* the fact she stuck her middle finger up at me. I mean, do nuns even *do* that? It was a second of staring at her, then she was off, and I was behind her, and that was that."

"You got enough information for the article from Sandy and Curmudgeon, I take it?"

"Yes, I'll be typing that up later. People will be asked to donate on the shelter's site — they've got a PayPal button in the sidebar. Hopefully, people will give enough cash to get that warehouse sorted. Sandy was saying that a supermarket manager is getting involved as well."

"I'll do a whip-round at the station when we get back, too," Mike said.

The rest of the day was taken up with paperwork and the usual crap that went with an investigation like this. At home time, no further forward, a plastic tub full of money from generous colleagues, they all went home.

What a fucking day.

CHAPTER SEVENTEEN

Shadwell always had been a shithole, but Dillon had nowhere else to go — nowhere he could get a bed pretty quickly anyway, unless he turned up at the shelter, but it was a bit too late in the day for that. The beds would already have been allocated, and it wasn't like they'd let him in for old time's sake, as though he was a mate they'd missed and wanted to catch up on the years he'd spent away.

He'd got himself into a bit of a pickle in York, where he'd gone after Zoe Paling had kicked him out, saying if he didn't go, she'd ring the police and tell them he'd broken in and killed Maggie. She'd had enough of him, that was what she'd said — enough of his 'dirty ways', whatever that had meant. It was her right, to tell him to leave, and he'd been getting tired of her always being pissed up, although her being in that state had helped him creep from their bed and into Leeanne's without Zoe questioning him. Zoe was only meant to be a stopgap anyway, and he'd really been there to visit Leeanne, so leaving hadn't been that much of a wrench. Leeanne had grown older, out of his age range, so it was handy he'd been forced to move on.

He'd missed the kid, though. He'd taught her to behave the right way with him, months of grooming, then the years that had followed, and she'd been like putty, hadn't she.

York had been all right at first. He'd paced the streets, working out who to avoid in the homeless community and who to approach. It was much the same in Shadwell, where there was a hierarchy, and he was at the bottom of the totem pole in this new place. Still, it was a challenge to work his way up, and in no time, he'd done the same to some woman as he'd done with Maggie, getting her to feel sorry for him, and then kipping at hers a couple of times a week.

She'd had a kid.

Problem was, that kid hadn't been as malleable as Leeanne, so he'd had to shelve that particular penchant of his and just stay at the house. No going into the girl's bedroom. He'd sensed right off the bat she'd be a squealer, running to Mummy to tell her 'that man' had touched her. Best to try elsewhere or just watch them playing at the park until a better option came along.

He'd drifted from there to several other homes over the years, chatting the women up in pubs after using begging money to wash his clothes in the laundrette and then pay to go swimming so he could have a good old soak in chlorine. He'd had to swim in his pants, but no one seemed to notice, and if they had, he wouldn't have given a shit. None of the women he'd charmed had any idea he was homeless, and that was the way he liked to play it.

It got you in the door, then your feet planted firmly under the table. He'd applied for Jobseeker's using the women's addresses, while they went out to work to bring home the money for the bills and food. He spent his on booze and fags, as it should be.

For years he'd hopped out of one bed and into another, and he'd reckoned he wouldn't find another Leeanne again until the final try, then there she'd been, the eight-year-old daughter of a twenty-something bird who'd just so happened to want a daddy figure for the pair of them. The mother, Yasmin, even called him Daddy instead of Dillon, which was a bit weird, but who was he to quibble about something so trivial when her little angel, Esme, liked his sausage.

Until she didn't like it. Until some stupid group or other had visited the school yesterday and told the children that their private parts were just that, private, and anyone touching them when they shouldn't was wrong, and it was against the law.

She'd whispered to him, last night, when his breath had been hot and he was all worked up, that she'd scream if he went near her again, that screaming was what the group had told her to do.

He didn't chance it. He'd left her room, grabbed his stuff, nicked the housekeeping money out of the biscuit tin in the kitchen, then fucked off to catch a train. Some of the readies were still in his pocket.

And once again, like he'd just thought, he muttered that Shadwell was a shithole, and coming back maybe wasn't his finest idea, but he'd been traipsing round all day, familiarising himself. He'd now go and see if Zoe was still about, see if she'd welcome him in like she'd done before. She'd be older, less attractive, but he wasn't exactly a bloody oil painting, was he, what with his overhanging belly from too much beer, and Leeanne, well, he imagined she'd have moved out by now, an adult, getting on with her own life. He'd sleep at Zoe's for a bit until he wheedled his way into a younger woman's affections — one who had a daughter — then he'd leave Zoe to it. Kick her to the kerb like she'd kicked him.

In the darkness, Maggie's place still stood proudly at the end of the snow-covered drive, and he stared up at the window he'd climbed in too many times to count. He remembered Leeanne pushing him off the fucking porch roof and how Maggie had whispered to him, when he'd been flat on his back, gravel biting into his arse, that she knew what he'd been doing, and if he ever came there again, she'd call the police.

A light glowed in that bedroom, and in his head, he saw the inside of it as it'd been back then, with the Barbie house in the corner, the doll asleep in the plastic bed. That Christmas had been ruined, Maggie buying him that stupid hat, gloves and scarf set, rubbing it in that he was homeless and he'd need them to ward off the cold on the nights she didn't let him stay there.

She was the one who'd turned cold in the end.

He laughed at the thought of how her body must have been cool to the touch when the doctor came to see her one last time. How that doc had pronounced Maggie's death as a heart attack, no questions asked, the stupid old codger.

Maybe Dillon ought to threaten Zoe now with the same fate as she'd given him — tell her if she didn't allow him inside, he'd let the coppers know *she'd* snuffed the old nun out. That'd make her behave.

He tromped up the drive and then knocked on the door. The same wreath hung from it, the bloody thing being brought out year after year — sentimental value, Leeanne had once said. Take the 'senti' off and just have 'mental', and that'd be the truth. How it had survived this long without falling apart he didn't know.

The door swung open, and Zoe stood there, still trim, although not as skinny as he remembered. Shit, she'd weathered the years well, and it put him on the back foot. He'd expected her to be frumpy, with a saggy gut to match his, grateful that someone — him — wanted her. Had she come into money and had surgery or what? She stared at him, eyes wide, mouth hanging open. So she was shocked at the sight of him then.

"Pleased to see me, are you?" he asked.

She stepped back, smiling a weird smile, and it unnerved him, like she knew something he didn't. He had to cover that unease up, act all manly and stuff. Get her to find him attractive.

"You look good," he said, thinking a compliment would go a long way to aiding his cause. Soften her up. "The years have been kind to you, Zoe."

She laughed, a proper belly jiggler, her head going back, her teeth displayed, and that was when he realised. The teeth. This wasn't Zoe but Leeanne, all grown up, the spit of her mother, and wasn't that a turn-up? He felt odd about it, about how he hadn't twigged and his mind had played a massive trick on him, but he'd soon get over that.

"You'd better come in," she said. "Can't have you being out there in the cold, can we. You don't have your hat, gloves and scarf set on."

He stepped inside, miffed at her dig, and eff me, that scarf Maggie had bought him hung from one of the coat hooks on the wall beside the pew. He closed the door, amazed that the hallway was exactly the same, and followed her into the kitchen. She went to the side where the kettle was — that was a new one — and flicked it on, the bugger sounding like it'd been boiled recently. Everything else was the same, though, right down to the cups dangling from the over-varnished mug tree. He'd walked back in time, and for a moment, it felt like he'd never left.

"Where's your mum?" He perched his arse at the table.

"Dead." She put a teabag in a cup.

You what? "Oh . . . I thought . . ."

"What did you think, Dillon?" She added sugar. Three.

She remembers how I take it. "I need a place to stay for a while. Thought Zoe would see me right."

"Why would she do that when she kicked you out?" The kettle finished boiling — *that was quick* — and she poured the water.

"I dunno. Thought we should let bygones be bygones. We're getting older, things change."

"Hmm, nice thought, but sometimes it doesn't work out that way, does it." She turned and handed him his tea. "I suppose you want something to eat, don't you?"

He nodded. "That'd be nice, very charitable of you. And, I don't want to sound rude, but can you put me up for the night? I'll get out of your hair tomorrow." *What a load of bullshit.*

"Okay." She swivelled and opened the fridge.

That surprised him, her agreeing to it. Maybe she'd missed him. Maybe she'd let him share her bed again. If he shut his eyes, he could pretend she was a kid. "Cheers."

While she cooked him a fry-up, he told her where he'd been, what he'd done — minus certain things, as he wouldn't want her to get jealous of the little girls he'd befriended

— and she made all the right noises, like she was listening and interested. She placed the food in front of him, same plate, same cutlery, and he dug in. She took the seat opposite and watched him scoff, that weird smile of hers coming back, giving him the willies.

"Lovely grub," he said then shovelled more in. "So how did your mum die?"

Didn't seem she liked him talking with his mouth full. Her grimace said so.

She closed her eyes for a moment. Opened them. Stared. "I don't want to discuss it."

"Ah, still painful, is it?" Cor, this bacon was nice and crispy.

She glared at him.

His cheeks heated.

"Would you like a second cup of tea?" she asked, the ice in her eyes melting.

He nodded, relieved the tense few seconds had passed. Shit, she looked like she had a temper on her these days. He'd need to tread carefully. "Yeah, thanks." He kept his attention on his food while she made the brew. Finishing a sausage, he wished he had a bit of bread and butter to mop up the bean juice. Best not to ask her for any, it'd be pushing it, and besides, he didn't fancy her staring at him again like she just had.

She put the tea on the table, and he drank it while she washed up, her back to him. He nosed about, content, and caught sight of a clear bottle by the tea canister, and it rang a bell, but he couldn't remember why. That was the problem with getting older. You tended to forget shit. He shrugged, and it seemed to take ages for his shoulders to go back down. Fuck me, he'd got tired all of a sudden.

"I'll be back in a second," she said.

Was she floating?

"All right." He folded his arms, closing his eyes. Just for a few minutes . . .

* * *

He woke to the sight of some woman standing in front of him, fingers to her temples, twisting her hands back and forth. Her face was so white apart from dark circles around her eyes, and her black lips, they were an angry slash. What was that all about then?

He frowned, taking in her hair and the clothes. They were Leeanne's, what she'd had on when she'd let him in. Was he having a bloody dream? He blinked and tried to lift his hand, but it didn't go very far, just rising a tad and then flopping back down. His muscles didn't seem to be working, and he felt so *heavy*.

"Where am I?" he croaked.

"You're in your room," the woman said, sounding the same as Leeanne. "I said you could stay here."

He glanced about. What was that all over the walls? Weird pictures, with blood drawn on the figures and ripped-out hearts or intestines. The men looked like the Devil. He blinked again, slowly, and managed to peer down at himself. He didn't have any clothes on — *what the hell?* — and was strapped to something or other, with a hard pole between his legs.

"Hungry again?" she asked.

He could do with another bite to eat as it happened, and he managed a nod.

"Good. I'll feed you what you fed me." She walked behind him, reappearing with a trolley. She took a metal dome off a plate and put it on her head. "Whatever happened to your camouflage helmet, Dillon?"

"Dunno," he slurred. "It got lost on my travels."

"Hmm."

The plate was empty, and that was a bit of a puzzle, one he had no energy to work out. How could she feed him with no food? A candy cane sat beside it, though, so he supposed she'd get him to eat that. Yeah, that was what she'd meant when she'd said she'd feed him what he'd fed her. He'd given her a peppermint cane that time, on the first night he'd . . .

He couldn't think straight. Every thought fragmented, scattering off into spiky pieces that gave him a headache.

She picked the cane up, and it glinted. Something was on the end of it, a blade maybe, and that was strange, wasn't it? She flashed it towards him, and it took him a moment to register the pain in his groin and the slap of something hitting the floor. He bent his head, and there was so much red coming out of him where his dick had once been. Then agony struck, sharp and brutal and gnawing and evil, and he screamed.

She stooped and picked up his penis, stood there staring at him with her head cocked until he stopped screeching. Then she stuffed it in his mouth.

"Does that taste good?" she asked.

The words were familiar. Ones he'd spoken to her many times before.

"Suck it until you choke," she said. Those words had also been his at one time, too, then she dropped the cane on the trolley and walked to the back of the room.

His groin throbbed, an ache he couldn't describe if he tried, and warm trickles slithered down his legs. Blood. He wanted to empty his mouth, but his tongue wouldn't work. It wouldn't expel his . . . his . . . oh God, she'd really sliced it off, hadn't she. Fuck. Shit!

She ran at him then, fast, her eyes malevolent slices, and kicked him in the head. His dick shot out of his gob, went flying, and he cried out, angry he couldn't fight back, even angrier there was nothing he could do to stop her.

"No! Let me do this, Stout Farmer!"

As she kicked some more, and punched, she told him how she felt about him coming into her room, how he'd wrecked her, tainted her mind, and turned her into this monster that she didn't really want to be. How she was Maggie, and him, and herself, and someone called Felicity Gray, all rolled into one, and my God, she hated him and herself.

He passed out.

CHAPTER EIGHTEEN

Leeanne washed the blood away using the hose and swept it all into the hole in the floor. She put his sausage on the plate, then took the dome off her head and covered the disgusting length of . . .

"Don't think about it," Felicity Gray said.

She untied the waist belt, and he fell to the stone slabs, still out of it from his beating and the magic potion in the glass bottle. She had such a good method of death for him, the new snowfall giving her the idea, plus one of those stupid 'challenges' the kids got up to these days. She hoped he'd wake up while it was in progress and feel the pain. If he didn't, so long as he died, that was all she really cared about. This was the *actual* Dillon, even her messed-up mind knew that, so she wouldn't have to keep going out into the streets in her Maggie form to find him after this. She'd come to the end, the last one, and she could live a peaceful life once all her demons had been slaughtered.

Gloves and habit on, she lugged him to the back garden and wrangled him into the passenger seat. Earlier, she'd protected it with a black bag tucked in so none of his silly blood left a stain. She strapped him in with the clingfilm seat belt, then checked the boot to make sure the weapons were still there. They were, loads of them, purchased with cash at several different shops, just an ordinary thing no one would bat an eyelid at.

It wouldn't kill him, but it would fucking hurt.

She drove him to the field closest to Shadwell Hill, where she parked by the woods in a field, then dragged the manky bastard by his wrists to just outside the tree line. God, he was heavy, and her back ached a bit. She dumped him down, returning to the car to collect her shovel and a tool bag with her other stuff in it. She scraped a body-shaped space in the snow, banking it up on one side. Pleased with her efforts, she dug the shovel in the mound then walked back and forth from the car to Dillon, carrying the weapons in their heavy bags, four or five at a time.

It took a while, and she got tired.

With him now in the carved-out space, not waking despite it being freezing — she'd thought the cold on his skin would have shocked him — she got to work, tying his wrists together, his ankles, then looping more rope from her tool bag between the bonds so the only movement he could achieve was bucking his pelvis or raising his head. She thought about the camping trip she'd gone on last year and took out tent pegs. Secured him to the ground with them via the ankle rope, annoyed she had to use a mallet to smack them into the unforgiving earth. The impact juddered her teeth.

Then she ripped open the plastic bags and poured the contents of one on his dickless groin, wishing he'd feel the sting of it on that open gash. She emptied the others all over his body. It took a while — there were a fair few, the biggest the supermarkets offered — and once she'd finished, she admired the calm before the storm, him oblivious. The salt was so thick on his stump that no blood was visible.

She grabbed the shovel and covered him in snow. Packed it down by whacking it. Laughing, crying, a sense of justice streaking through her. Felicity screamed at her to stop. Despair came, too, because now she'd got him, the right

Dillon, what would she focus on afterwards? How would she even live? Could she go back to how she'd been after Mother had died, when she'd been happy and had passed as a 'normal' human being?

Thoughts for tomorrow.

She stood and waited. For what seemed like ages.

The cold snow would send that salt even colder, and the heat from his skin cells, well, it'd be soaking up the salt-and-snow mixture, creating second- then third-degree burns. She'd read all about it. That had to be hurting by now, but with him out of it, all that pain was going to waste . . .

She switched on her phone torch and aimed the beam at his face. Oh, he was waking. How exciting. Eyelids fluttering. Lips twitching. A frown forming. She quickly stuffed three of the empty salt bags in his mouth to muffle any screams, pushing hard to clog his throat. Okay, it was late, or early hours if you wanted to be exact about it, but some nutter might be out there walking their dog. You never could predict the lunacy of some people, could you.

As she'd expected, he bucked, but only a little, that second cup of tea keeping his limbs heavy. Some of the snow cracked, a crevasse in the Antarctic, threatening to expose his salt-caked body. She positioned her phone on one of the bags against a mini snow hillock so it illuminated his face, then snatched up the shovel and patted the snow down again, hard, his garbled screams sounding like his throat was getting sore already.

Blimey, such a fuss . . .

Snow came away from his neck as he managed to lift his head a couple of inches. The cords on his neck strained and his teeth clenched, the bags hidden behind them. He snorted, eyes bulging where he fought to breathe through his nostrils.

She'd had enough of his daft behaviour.

She raised the shovel and brought it down on his disgusting face, over and over again, blood spatter creating pretty dotted patterns on the white blanket around him, probably behind her, too, flying over her head with each reverse arc.

Out of breath, she stopped and wondered if he was out of breath yet, too. She couldn't tell. His face was wrecked, mush, like the raw meat she'd fed the others, and it wasn't like she could see his chest rising and falling, was it. Cleaning the shovel in the snow, she piled more on top of him so he was a pristine white mountain, his face secreted beneath it, too, so she didn't have to look at the mangy twazzock.

Once she'd covered the surrounding blood as well, she slid her phone into her pocket, slung her tool bag over her shoulder and, walking backwards, swung the shovel over the snow in arcs to obliterate her footprints and the blood. She left the empty salt bags there, generous in letting the police know how he'd been burnt. It'd save them the headache of working it out.

Her Christmas present to them.

Shovel and bag in the boot, she got in the car and waited a while for the heater to warm her up, then she was off, travelling home, where she bleached The Room and cleaned the whole ground floor, as well as the car to remove any traces of him. His sausage, though . . . Maybe she'd keep that. No firm decision there.

She burned the black bag from the passenger seat, the clingfilm from the seat belt, his ID, clothes, shoes, the habit and her gloves in the large oil drum in the back garden. She wouldn't be giving the police a head start as to who he was by leaving his identification behind. Not this time. They'd follow his life trail back to her. He'd lived with them, and there'd be a record of it. She stared at the flames in the darkness, at the dancing, blackened flecks, smoke tickling her throat, and smiled her Maggie smile mixed with a touch of Leeanne.

She went inside, flicked the kettle on and looked at the magic bottle. She was grateful to it for being her partner in crime.

An hour or so later after a warming coffee, with the sun trying valiantly, but failing, to break through the wintery sky, dawn struggling to shift her arse out of her airy bed to greet another day, Leeanne took her Maggie makeup off for the last time, then showered, the stench of smoke in her hair replaced with the lush scent of TRESemmé. In her fleece pyjamas — no need for Maggie's nighties anymore — and fluffy slippers and dressing gown, she took a flask of tea down to the caravan and sat on the U-shaped seating with Mr Teddy, watching the morning come alive, birds chirping, and she sipped, thinking, hoping her life could be what it would have been had she not been treated the way she had. A good life, one without pain, but the thought, as cold as the snow and the crisp nip in the air, reminded her that memories would still be with her, so she'd never truly be free.

And she'd left her mallet behind.

Shit. That was a pisser.

* * *

Pam McDonnell was up with the lark, jogging through the woods, her Yorkies, Bella and Max, gallivanting off ahead, their ears flapping. They barked, excited, calling for her to hurry up, to catch them so she could throw the little ball they'd just chased after. She laughed, speeding up, while they waited patiently, the ball now in Max's mouth. He dropped it upon her approach, and she picked it up as she sailed past. She lobbed it again, and the bloody thing hit a trunk at the tree line and then shot off out into the snow-covered field. Bella and Max legged it, and she pursued, her smile hurting her face. She loved those silly doggies.

There wasn't much snow in the woods, the evergreens tall and bushy, preventing the majority of it from falling through the branches, so when she ran out onto the snow, the change beneath her feet took a moment to get used to.

The dogs were to the right, digging away. The ball must have landed in that mound.

"Find it then," she said, walking, her breaths coming out in grey puffs. "Then we need to go back. I've got to go to work." Why she'd told them that, she didn't know. They couldn't answer her. Still, she liked having a natter with them all the same.

Bella and Max dug on. Christ, that ball must have burrowed deep.

"Come on," she called. "We need to go."

Max stopped pawing and looked at her over his shoulder, barked, and carried on ferreting. That bark . . . Something was wrong.

She crunched over the snow, which was oddly packed down, as though someone had purposely flattened it. Pawprints had marred strange arc patterns. Pam frowned and cautiously made her way to the mound.

Why was some of the snow pink? Had one of the dogs hurt themselves?

"Bella, Max," she said, her tone sharp so they'd stop mucking about with their digging so she could check their faces. They might have scratched their snouts on a branch or something.

They ignored her.

Closer she went, pink snow going flying as the dogs swept it away. A slushie drink, strawberry.

She moved her hand to her jogger bottoms pocket, unzipping it to withdraw her phone. A feeling of dread seeped into her. She moved nearer and made out a volcano-like crater Max had made, the lava inside some kind of . . . *mangled flesh*?

"Oh, bloody hell. Shit!"

Heart thudding, she whipped her phone up to her face. Hands shaking, she jabbed in her passcode to unlock it.

"Get away," she snapped.

They didn't.

She brought up her number pad and prodded in nine-nine-nine, about to tell herself it would just be some wild animal, injured, the snow coming down to freeze it to death.

Until Bella's speedy paws whipped more snow away and revealed hands on top of the lava, the wrists tied with rope.

"No," she shouted, grabbing the dogs' tails to tug them and let him know they *had* to come away.

"What's your emergency?" a woman said on the other end of the line.

"A body," Pam managed. "I think my dogs have found a body."

CHAPTER NINETEEN

"It's all very well," Bethany said, "being up at this time of the morning because I choose to, but being called out before eight when our shift hasn't even started — again . . ."

"They can't bloody help it, can they." Mike secured his seat belt. "The dead buggers have no say in whether their bodies getting discovered messes up our day. I'm sure they'd rather be alive and, you know, looking forward to Christmas. The shelter puts on food Christmas and Boxing Day — that's if this body is a homeless person."

"I know. Ignore me. I'm a grumpy cow." She pulled away and headed for Shadwell Hill. "But along with getting no sleep because this sodding case is going around and around in my head, we haven't got a chance to ease into our day and have a meeting to see what we should do next, because another body has been found. Who walks their dogs at arse o'clock?"

"People who like to make sure their pets have a run before being cooped inside all day? Anyway, like you just advised, I'm ignoring you." Mike lifted the coffee she'd made him from the cup holder. Sipped. "Lovely. Lots of sugar."

"And it's shit that . . ." She stopped. No, she was *not* going to moan about Vinny not being here and her spending

Christmas alone. She thought she'd come to terms with it the other day, but obviously not. Mike didn't need to hear her shit. God knew how much he'd listened to already since Vinny had died. "Right, subject change. What did you watch on the telly last night? Anything interesting?"

"I binged a few episodes of *Unbelievable*. I'll finish it tonight if we manage to get home on time. I was meant to catch it when it first came on Netflix, but with work and whatever . . ."

"What's it about?"

"You don't want to know. You'll get upset. It's one of my usual shows."

"Ah, detectives?"

"Hmm."

She took him at his word and didn't press for more. If he said she'd get upset, she'd rather not hear about it. "So, we may as well discuss work then. Ursula said, when she rang me, that this might be one of ours. The body was packed in the snow like the last one."

"We didn't get any fresh fall during the night, so it must have been deliberately put beneath it."

"*If* it was put there last night or in the early hours. Who knows, it could have been dumped before the latest fall."

"There is that, but if so . . . Doesn't matter."

"Spit it out."

"I was just going to say why hadn't someone found it before now, but with this weather, I doubt there's many who would brave it to go to the woods with their dog."

"Except the woman who found the body. Pam McDonnell. Well, her dogs found it. Dug part of it up, apparently. Nice crime scene fuckup."

"Not the dogs' fault . . . or hers." Mike sipped.

"No. Shame we've got a contaminated scene, though." She drove down the main road beside the hill, careful of the snow. The gritters hadn't been out this far, so it was pretty treacherous. It seemed to have frozen overnight, none of that nice powdery stuff but squashed down from tyres.

"Isabelle and her lot are here then." Mike pointed to the left.

A tent had been erected just outside the tree line in the distance, and a SOCO van was parked about one hundred metres away from the main scene, as was a patrol car. With the sky still gloomy at seven in the morning, dawn fighting to show her face, the tent was lit up from within by a halogen, a box of yellow-white light with a pointed roof. Bethany just made out SOCOs milling around, their suits meshing with the white surroundings.

She turned left onto the field and followed the tyre tracks the SOCO van had made, then came to a stop behind it. The van doors were open at the back, so they got out and took protective clothing from inside a cardboard box, getting togged up while a stiff, evil wind decided to wallop them about a bit, the charming bastard.

They trudged along a trench made from SOCOs' boots and approached Tory, who stood bundled up, a hi-vis on top of her black police coat, a scarf double-wrapping her neck, covering her chin. It brought the nun to mind, and Bethany shivered. Had that bitch been out here under the cover of darkness?

While they signed the log, Bethany asked, "Where's the lady who called us?"

"In the back of the patrol car," Tory said. "With her dogs." She winced. "Getting their snowy paws and fur on my upholstery."

Bethany smiled. "Glad it isn't just me who's a mardy bugger this morning."

"Oh, you, too?" Tory slid the log into her pocket.

"Unfortunately, yes." Bethany sighed. "We'll talk to the woman first. Did you get anything out of her?"

"A load of babbling, to be honest." She lowered her voice. "It's too early for me to be dealing with that gumph, so I told her to sit in the car to calm down."

"Right. Great." Bethany turned to look at the car and felt sorry for the poor cow who stared out at her, eyes red-rimmed.

"Let's get this sorted so she can go home. Must have been one hell of a shock."

"Glen and Tammy are over the other side of the woods," Tory said. "Where Pam McDonnell left her car."

"Okay."

She led Mike to the patrol, and he got in the passenger side, Bethany in the driver's seat, and she faced the back, introducing them while Mike got his notebook and pen out.

"Pam McDonnell?" Bethany smiled at the dogs, who'd lolloped their hairy bodies across the woman's lap.

"Yes." Pam nodded.

"Tell me what happened from the start."

Pam related her story, stroking her dogs — Bella and Max, she'd said.

"Did you see anyone or a vehicle around when you arrived?" Bethany asked.

Pam shook her head. "No, I parked up on the other side of the woods. Absolutely no one about, and to be honest, it felt a bit scary, like I was the only one in the world, but I soon forgot that once I started jogging."

"Did you notice any tyre tracks where you left your car?"

"No, but there were some on the field. I spotted that after, when I had more time to look around. One set in and out, so I just thought someone else had been in the woods with their dog earlier on, but I didn't see a soul."

"Okay. So you didn't see anyone watching you when Bella and Max discovered the body?"

Pam shivered. "Oh God, do you think they were? It didn't even enter my head. I was so wrapped up with the blood and the hands . . ."

"No, whoever did this is long gone."

"So they won't have spotted my car and know who I am?" Pam patted Max.

"I doubt it. If you only saw tyre tracks . . . Any footprints? Pawprints?"

"I didn't notice."

"I don't think you have anything to worry about." Bethany asked for her address and phone number and then passed her card over. "If you think of anything else, ring me. Someone will call round over the next day or two for a proper statement, but to be honest, with Christmas so close, it might be afterwards. Would you like an escort back to your car?"

Pam nodded. "Please."

They all got out, and Bethany spoke to a SOCO, who was more than happy to take Pam. Other officers were in the woods, searching for evidence, and he said he'd join them afterwards.

"You might find a ball," Pam said to Bethany. "I threw it, and it must have landed in that . . . that mound, which is why the dogs dug at it. It's yellow."

"Okay, don't worry about that. Go home and have a sweet cup of tea. Do you have someone who can sit with you? It's been a shock."

"I'll ask my neighbour to pop round."

Pam walked off with the SOCO, Bella and Max trotting along beside her. Bethany and Mike plodded ahead to the tent, passing SOCOs using rakes over the snow and putting it into large plastic boxes. Bethany took a deep breath and then entered, greeted by Isabelle, who stood to one side while a photographer, on his knees, took close-ups of what appeared to be someone's mangled groin. He got up and took up his task in another area of the tent.

"We have a dickless wonder," Isabelle said, pointing to where it would have been.

"Pack it in, you." Bethany walked closer. Dear God, what a sight. "Those dogs actually scrabbled in that mess."

"Hmm." Isabelle nodded. "We've swabbed their paws and scraped their claws. I assume the snow got the rest off when they went to Tory's car."

"She's going to go mental if she finds body matter on her back seat," Mike said. "She was already moaning about the fur."

"Best we don't let her in on it then." Isabelle smiled, conspiratorial, the cheeky bugger. "So, someone's annoyed about this man's willy enough to cut it off, which suggests he did things with it he shouldn't."

Anger burned inside Bethany. While she couldn't condone this . . . She'd want to chop off someone's todger as well if they used it on her without permission.

"Why only remove this bloke's, though?" Mike asked. "If the killer is fixated on someone who hurt her, and she's selecting people similar to him, why not lop all their cocks off?" He winced. "Was that done . . . ?"

"While he was alive?" Isabelle finished for him. "What do you think? The amount of blood . . ."

Mike plaited his legs. "Fucking hell. That had to have killed."

"Well, if that didn't, the bags in his mouth did."

"I didn't mean it that way, like the removal killed him," he said.

"I know." Isabelle grinned. "Just being my usual pedantic self. You know you love it."

"Whatever you want to think, Izz. Whatever gets you through the day, my friend." Mike chuckled.

"Uh, have you two kiddies finished?" Bethany smiled. She hadn't noticed the bags in the victim's mouth so leant forward. His teeth were only slightly parted, but plastic was inside. "And you know it's a bag because?"

Isabelle scooped an evidence sack out of a box. "These were lying around. Salt bags. Loads of them."

"Salt?" Bethany frowned.

"And a mallet." Isabelle popped the first sack away then took out another, transparent, the mallet in clear view. No blood on it.

"Used to smash his head in then cleaned?" Mike said.

"That's for Presley to determine." Isabelle put the sack in the box. "But I can't see any rectangular indents on his barnet, can you?"

Mike shook his head. "No."

Presley, as though he'd heard her mention his name, hustled in, coming to stand at the bottom of the mound. "Crikey, someone didn't like him. What a state."

"We haven't found ID like before either," Isabelle said. "We've raked back the surrounding snow, and no clothes, no note, only the dog ball, so is it the same killer? What with the willy being missing . . ."

"I can see that." Presley instinctually went to cup his own and must have realised he was in company. He gripped his bag with two hands instead. "Such pain . . . He's got burns, too. That exposed skin . . . see the blisters? Some have been popped." He shuddered, which was unusual for him. Perhaps it was the lack of a penis that had got to him, not the body.

"Um, dogs decided to dig him up, hence the blisters popping," Isabelle said.

He put his bag down. "That's unfortunate. Right, the last one was flame burn, but this is different."

"There were empty salt bags left on the scene if that helps," Isabelle said.

"Ah, yes." Presley nodded. "Salt lowers the temperature at which ice melts — snow in this case. So, most definitely frostbite. Salt on the skin first, the snow packed on, temp going down to minus twenty-one degrees Celsius, causes the blisters, and that equals third-degree burns. You get the picture. Had he lived, that would have scarred, and he'd have had an excruciating recovery period."

"How would you know to do this sort of shit, though? Are we after a scientist or what?" Bethany asked.

"The salt-and-ice challenge," Presley said. "Stupid children doing stupid things. It gets put on the internet, then the general public find out about it. Maybe our woman saw it online and thought about the snow. Quite a bit of salt must have been used."

"I haven't got a definite number because there are salt bags in his mouth," Isabelle said. "But we picked up seventeen of them off the ground."

"Right, well, if I'm free to take a look?" Presley cocked his head at Isabelle.

"Yes, fine by me."

"The body temperature is going to royally mess up the estimated time of death," he grumbled, going down on his knees. He took a pair of tweezers from his bag. "I don't even know if I'll be able to get the bag of salt out because of rigor." He pulled down the jaw. "A bit stiff, probably from the cold. That groin wound and the face wreckage looks pretty fresh, so we're talking overnight, not him being buried under the snow for days." He tugged at the bag. Then another and another. "So three, which makes twenty." He glanced up at Bethany.

"If she bought them all at the same time, she's pretty stupid." Bethany gave in, even though she didn't want her team awake early, and sent a message to Leona, again telling her to leave Fran to spend time with her child. She also related what had happened, then:

Bethany: SO I NEED YOU TO GET THE CCTV ON THE ROADS LEADING TO SHADWELL HILL—I KNOW THERE AREN'T MANY, BUT WE NEED TO DO IT ANYWAY, OBVIOUSLY. ALSO LOOK INTO THE SUPERMARKETS AND SEE IF ANYONE BOUGHT BAGS OF SALT. COULD BE ONE AT A TIME, COULD BE SEVERAL IN DIFFERENT STORES. BASICALLY, ASK IF THERE'S BEEN A RECENT UPSURGE IN SALES OF IT. I CAN'T SEE MANY PEOPLE BUYING IT IN BIG BAGS VERY OFTEN, CAN YOU? IT'S JUST TABLE SALT, NOTHING TO DO WITH GETTING RID OF SNOW. CHEERS.

Leona: I MUST HAVE KNOWN. I GOT UP EARLY. SEE YOU LATER.

Bethany: TTFN!

She slid her phone away.

"So with no ID," Mike was saying, "and no facial features to go on, this is going to be harder. What about a weapon for the face?"

"Something hard and flat," Presley said. "Probably the shovel used to dig the snow. And as for no identification, there's a tattoo. A rather tacky one, I might add, on the side of his neck. An amateur did it, I'd say. Maybe he did it himself with ink and a compass while looking in a mirror. It's got the feel of a homemade one about it."

"What's it of?" Bethany asked.

"Hard to see well, what with the blood, but it appears to be the words CANDY GIRL, plus a candy cane." Presley shrugged. "Ugly thing."

Bethany had a peek. The ink had a dark-green tinge, and the edges of the letters and the cane bled out, reminiscent of an unprofessional giving it a go.

"So if he's homeless, that's something he'll be recognised by," Mike said.

"A trip to see Sandy and Curmudgeon, I think," Bethany said.

"That's if this fella gave out his real name." Mike folded his hands under his armpits.

"Indeed. Well, we're off then." Bethany smiled at Isabelle and then Presley.

"Oh, a little bird told me the tox results from Karl Hartley," Presley said. "Unofficially. He'll be sending them in later today. Carisoprodol, diazepam, trimipramine . . . All of them combined could knock someone out in certain doses. Causes numb limbs, slow speech. Carisoprodol is specifically a muscle relaxer, so make of that what you will."

"Perhaps they were used to keep the victims compliant while they were being held," Bethany said.

"If all of them have the same in their system . . ." Mike grimaced.

"Hmm, we'll look into it as if they do. Let's go."

On the way to the car, she sent another message to Leona about the drugs. Had someone been prescribed them? Or were they bought on the black market, or from some scumbag on a street corner? It wasn't unheard of for homeless people to be on drugs, and it didn't have to be coke or heroin either. Prescription stuff was just as damaging if not taken properly. A lot to mull over.

Someone, somewhere, had supplied a killer and unknowingly aided them in committing murder. If a doctor, doing this innocently, she dreaded to think of the burden the guilt would heap on them if details of this leaked out, even though it wasn't their fault.

Life, at times, really did play on without a care, dragging people into its wicked game — whether they wanted to be a part of it or not.

CHAPTER TWENTY

Leeanne had napped for a couple of hours in the caravan, snug beneath the patchwork quilt, waking to a murky sky loaded with more snow just waiting to float down. Everything appeared in degrees of grey outside the frosty-at-the-edges window, except for the snow, only marred by car tyre tracks and her footsteps to the van.

She could look forward to Christmas in a couple of days now, and while she'd be alone, with no presents beneath the tree, it was preferable to having her memories and hatred keeping her company. She'd given herself a gift already.

And the gift is murder.

Christmas. It brought back memories. Terrible, terrible memories.

But they seemed to have almost vanished now, along with the real Dillon. She remembered what she had to do, the last thing, then she'd be truly free.

Leaving Mr Teddy resting under the patchwork quilt, she traipsed up the garden, sneaky snow getting inside her slippers, melting against her warm feet. In the house, she put them upside down on the radiator in the hallway to dry, then dipped downstairs to The Room, where she'd left the trolley, the dome and the sausage underneath.

Shivering at the sight of the images she'd drawn on the walls in her frenzies, when her mind hadn't been her own, when she was the Leeanne who'd hurt anyone and everyone who resembled Dillon, she couldn't believe they'd been created by her hand, her twisted mind. Such anger in the charcoal strokes, and all that blood . . .

What had happened to her? Where had her head and heart sent her? And what was she supposed to do now? *Could* she move on from this?

Lost and somewhat lonely, standing there with her new self and trying desperately to fit inside the old, she blinked.

Maggie. It had all been her fault, not Christmas's. She'd let Mother in, with that tiny newborn baby in the carrier bag. She'd let Dillon in, too, with that disgusting thing in his pants. What would the alternative have been like? Would Mother have given Leeanne up to Social Services, leaving her to a life of endless foster parents, some who may have loved her, some who undoubtedly wouldn't? Or would she have abandoned Leeanne in that bag by the supermarket wheelie bin, to die alone, the plastic perhaps sticking to her face with every inhale as she'd screamed, for milk, for a cuddle and comfort, eventually killing her? Would it have been preferable to what she'd been through?

She couldn't comprehend ever living with anyone else but Maggie, Mother and Dillon. It was all she knew, except for the fake life she'd made up in her head when he'd—

No. Go away.

Her days had been a nightmare, and so had the dark hours. Her whole existence was blighted at some point every single day. Could be morning, could be afternoon, but it was always the evening. Mother, bullying. Dillon, touching. She couldn't recall a day when she hadn't had something happen to knot her stomach, Leeanne biting her bottom lip hard to stop herself from crying.

The life of the abused — terrifying, secluded, isolating.

'If you tell anyone, I'll kill you . . .'

'Let me just put it there, Candy Girl . . .'

'What does it taste like?'

Now she lived alone.

She carried the dome-covered plate and the candy cane upstairs and placed them on the worktop. The glass bottle snagged her attention, and she reached for it, unscrewing the lid, pouring the contents down the sink and pretending all her worries had gone down there with it. That magic potion wasn't needed now, and the homeless men of Shadwell could rest easy tonight, as could she.

Leeanne lifted the dome and stared at the thing that had hurt her so many times, invaded her, sending her to a secret place in her head where she pretended she lived on a farm with gambolling lambs and fluffy yellow chicks. Where the sun was on her face and warming the top of her head, her mother a cheery, portly baker who made cakes for the villagers, her father the stout farmer, green wellies on his feet, all covered in cow shit, and even the filth of that was better than the filth at home.

A dream. A need. A yearning.

One she'd never attained, except when she went there in her head.

She put the *thing* in the blender, minus the end, the ugly head — she'd work out what to do with that later. Lid screwed on tight, she switched the machine on. That wicked piece of flesh churned around, the blades slicing it up, creating mush. She poured it down the sink, too, with running water, so it flowed into the sewer with the magic potion and the wisps of her shoddy upbringing, never to be seen or thought of again. She cleaned up, put the blender away, and bleached everywhere — the worktops, the sink, the table, the floor. Reverently, she took the cane into the living room and hung it on the Christmas tree, front and centre, a reminder of how the nightmare with Dillon had started — and how it had ended.

She turned on the fairy lights, and it was as though a night sky had come inside, settling in the corner, the lights the stars, pinpricks of hope, and she no longer had to pray for a shooting one where she could wish upon it, not asking for pretty shoes, dolls, or a fancy party dress, but a new life, one without heartache, misery and a tummy constantly taut.

Happiness. It had arrived at last.

CHAPTER TWENTY-ONE

Bethany parked outside the shelter. It was closing in on quarter to eight, and a few homeless people came out, bleary-eyed, some with backpacks, some with carrier bags, and all with hot drinks in beige plastic cups. They clomped off in the hard-packed snow for another day of walking the streets of Shadwell, one of them skidding, beverage slopping over the cup rim to land as a brown splodge in the whiteness at his feet.

"Poor sod," she muttered, getting her phone out. Her message alert had gone off just as she'd killed the engine.

> Leona: CCTV HAS A FEW DARK VEHICLES AND ONE WHITE HEADING IN THE DIRECTION OF THE ROAD THAT LEADS TO SHADWELL HILL IN THE TIME FRAME WE NEED, BUT OF COURSE, I CAN'T SEE ANYTHING CONCRETE. ON THE OTHER HAND, ONE SUPERMARKET, THE ONE WHERE THE BODY HAD BEEN DUMPED, HAD A SINGLE SALE OF FIVE BAGS OF SALT YESTERDAY. I'LL KEEP GOING WITH THE OTHER SHOPS.

Bethany: OKAY, CAN YOU GET FRAN ONTO TATTOOS. I WANT A SEARCH DONE ON ALL PEOPLE ARRESTED WITHIN THE LAST TWO YEARS WHO HAS ONE. THE TATTOO WE'RE AFTER IS A PICTURE OF A CANDY CANE, LIKE YOU EAT AT CHRISTMAS, AND THE WORDS: CANDY GIRL.

Leona: OKIE DOKIE.

Bethany: THANKS.

"Let's nip round the back and see if Curmudgeon is still in the warehouse first," Bethany said, glancing across at Mike. "Who knows if he gets fed his breakfast before everyone else and sets off early. If anyone will remember a tattoo like that, it's him."

They got out and walked down the side of the shelter. All evidence of a body and the police being there had gone, apart from the trodden-down snow. The warehouse door inched open, and a straggly fella came out, followed by Curmudgeon, who ambled towards them, the top of his backpack peeking over his head. He lifted a gloved hand in greeting, pausing to let the other man go ahead.

"Morning," Bethany said.

Curmudgeon nodded. "It's a cold one. I'm just off to pick up my breakfast."

"We'll come with you," she said. "I've got a question to ask, so maybe Sandy will let us talk in her office. You can get warmed up then, too."

In the shelter, Curmudgeon led the way to the dormitory and through a door to another room. A large hatch was open, and women served food and hot drinks. Sandy, looking tired and in need of her bed after the night shift, smiled as they approached.

"Let me just say," Sandy said, excitement palpable, "that as of this morning, we have four thousand and twenty-three pounds towards renovating the warehouse. It came in through PayPal via the website during the night. Angela from *The Herald* managed to get an evening slot on the local radio — she's such a lovely woman. It's more than I ever could have imagined, and we can buy even more beds and blankets. I'm so pleased."

"That's brilliant," Bethany said, so happy more homeless would have warm beds.

"I've got four hundred-odd from the station whip-round," Mike said. "I'll nip it in when we're not rushed off our feet."

"My God," Sandy said, smile wide. "This is unbelievable." Then she frowned. "Um, why are you here?"

Bethany raised her eyebrows.

"Oh no . . ." Sandy glanced from her to Mike to Curmudgeon. "We'll go to my office."

"I'm getting me nosh," Curmudgeon said. "Otherwise these grasping bleeders will eat my portion."

"We'll wait," Bethany said.

Once his polystyrene tray held a bacon roll and he clutched a plastic cup full of stewed tea, they walked out and into the dorm, where someone was busy stripping off the pillowcases ready for washing. Up the corridor, they turned into Sandy's office, and she closed the door, immediately going over to the coffeemaker to pour drinks. Curmudgeon settled on a chair to eat his roll, accepting another cuppa to go along with his tea.

"Okay, to be frank, we have another body," Bethany said, "only this time, we have no ID or clothing left behind. However, he did have a tattoo, and we were wondering if it might ring any bells."

"What is it?" Crumbs clung to Curmudgeon's beard, his lips shiny with margarine.

She told him, and his eyes widened.

"Bloody hell, where's *he* been all this time then?" He bit a chunk of roll.

Sandy gave Mike a coffee.

"Who?" Bethany said.

"There's only one person I know with a tattoo like that." Curmudgeon managed to talk and eat without it looking gross. "And that's Dillon Orton, the pervy little bastard."

Bethany's mind spun. *The lack of a penis. Pervy. Candy Girl — could that be some sick pet name?* She swallowed, clutching the coffee Sandy handed her. "Thank you." She sipped some.

"Yeah, he's a kiddie fiddler, that one. Only girls, mind. Makes you sick, doesn't it?" Curmudgeon took a swig of his tea. "Ruddy 'eck, that's hot, that is. I'm going to get a blister on the roof of me mouth."

"What do you know of him, this Dillon?" Bethany looked at Mike, glad to see he already had his phone out, tapping away one-handed at a message for Fran or Leona.

"He's a weird one." Curmudgeon coughed. "Sometimes he's homeless, sometimes he isn't. Like, he manages to find women to let him stay at their places — women with little girls — so for months at a stretch you don't see him, then when he's been kicked out, back he comes to the shelter. A bad penny. Not seen him for years."

"I can vouch for that," Sandy said. "The coming and going, I mean. I didn't know he was . . . was someone like *that*. If I had, I wouldn't have let him stay here."

"He told me all this when he was drunk on Stella one night, didn't he," Curmudgeon said, then stuffed the last of his breakfast in his mouth. He chewed. Swallowed. "Stayed with this one woman for yonks, he did, but I'll be blowed if I can remember where, though. She had a daughter."

"Did he ever tell you the daughter's name?" Bethany's heart thudded, hollow thumps that hurt her chest, her lungs going tight.

"Yeah, Anne or something."

"What about the woman?"

"Chloe." He scratched his head. "Or maybe it wasn't. I tended to switch off when he was yakking. Best I didn't know everything he got up to, although I did ring you lot about him once, so he might be on your system. I told the copper he was a nonce. Dunno if anything came of it, though. It's not something he'd likely have spoken about while sober, you know, admitting the coppers had pulled him in. He was a soldier for a while, or so he said. Used to walk about with a camouflage helmet on. Looked a right dick, if you ask me."

"Okay, thank you very much, but we have to go. Sorry I didn't drink all the coffee, Sandy." Bethany placed it beside Curmudgeon's cup.

"I'll have that," he said, grinning. Then he sobered. "Dead, is he?"

Bethany nodded. "We're assuming it's him, yes."

"Good." He patted his heart. "Scum like that don't deserve a life."

They said goodbye and rushed to the car. Mike didn't receive a return message on the way to the station, so they barrelled into the incident room, converging on Fran and Leona, bringing with them the crisp scent of a winter day.

"Got anything?" Bethany asked.

"I was just about to ring you." Fran consulted her screen. "Dillon Orton's on the system — small things like theft and whatever after he left the army. Last known address is in York — he was on jobseeker's, claiming from the home of a Yasmin Graham, who has a daughter, Esme, aged seven."

"Shit," Mike said, getting his phone out. "I'll get hold of the police there so they can go and visit, see if that little one is all right."

"What's happened?" Leona said, frowning.

"Curmudgeon said Orton is a fiddler. Girls." Bethany felt sick.

"Fuck," Fran said. "Okay, he's had a few homes in York, not for long, though, and they all have daughters. Here, Mike, the names and addresses." She handed them over. "But the most interesting thing is, after he left the army, he was homeless but ended up staying at Maggie James' for a good few years after her death."

"What?" Bethany's blood ran cold. "With Zoe and Leeanne Paling?" She thought of the names Curmudgeon had given her — Anne and Chloe. The old sod hadn't quite got them right, but they were close enough for her.

"Yes," Fran said. "From when Leeanne was quite small — again, he claimed unemployment benefit from there."

"It was her all along?" Bethany said. "The black car, the habit . . . Mike, leave that to Leona, will you? We need to get round to that bloody nunnery."

They shot out of the station, Bethany almost going arse over tit in the car park, and she held back a shout of frustration. They'd been to that woman's house, had spoken to her, and while she'd been fucking weird, nothing else had stood out as it being her — nothing they could use anyway. Maybe it *wasn't* her, but the coincidence was far too big for Bethany to ignore this, plus her instincts pushed her to drive as fast as the snow allowed so they could get to the nunnery before the crazy bitch did anything else.

She parked on the street outside, blocking the drive. They stood on the doorstep, knocking, Bethany telling herself to calm the hell down. She couldn't go in there all accusing, and she'd need to act professional in order to get the woman to slip up.

Mike stepped to the side to peer through the front window. "Christmas tree lights are on. Too dark beyond that to see anyone inside, though."

With no one answering the sodding door, she whispered, "You stay here. I'll go and look round the back."

She stole down the side of the house, walking in tyre tracks, which set off her inner alarm. Tyre tracks. But there had been no car in the garage. What the hell was going on?

At the rear corner, she peered round into the garden.

A black Vectra was parked by the back door.

"Christ Almighty . . ."

She looked away, scoping out the rest of the area. Footsteps went ahead from where Bethany stood, some toes facing the van, others facing her, so someone had gone down there and come back again. An old-fashioned caravan sat at the bottom, naked tree branches curved over the roof in the shape of a skeletal, protective hand. A candle burned in the small window to the left, and she reversed, keeping her sights on it, and, back at the front, clicked her finger and thumb to get Mike's attention.

He came to her side.

"Vectra in the garden. And a wooden caravan thing," she said. "I think someone's in it — if not, they're bloody stupid to leave a candle alight in there."

"Backup?" he asked.

"Not yet, we're just asking questions at the moment. We've got nothing but suspicions."

"But what if she kicks off?"

"There is that."

They walked ahead, reaching the caravan, and Bethany let out a long breath.

"It's a fucking fake candle," she said. "One of those battery-operated efforts. Can't see anyone in there, can you?" She stared at a U-shaped seating area, a patchwork quilt with a teddy bear's head poking out of it on the side closest to her.

Mike moved to the other window on the right. Peered in. "Nope."

"Back to the house then."

At the door, Mike hammered on it, the wreath lifting then falling with each smack he gave. He peeked through the letterbox. "Oh fuck . . ."

"What? *What?*" Bethany's heart skittered, and she bent over, nudging him out of the way to look through the slot.

A black scarf with beige stripes hung on a hook.

She straightened up, letting the flap close. "Now *that* isn't a coincidence. Okay, backup is needed now; I'm too uneasy. Plus, she was well weird when we saw her, and I don't fancy her going funny on us. I was stupid to say we'd handle this on our own."

They retreated to her car. Mike rang the station while Bethany had a sudden thought. She took some gloves and booties out of the box on the back seat, put them on, then pointed to the rear garden, mouthing: *Vectra*. Slim flashlight in hand, she was ready to go nosing. Mike nodded, gesturing that he'd keep an eye on the house, and she jogged down the drive as best she could, keeping her legs stiff in her attempt not to slip over. At the Vectra, she used her torch, shining the beam inside.

A spot of what looked like blood had seeped into the side of the passenger seat.

Fucking got you.

On a whim, and with no one watching from inside the house as far as she could see, she walked round and tried the driver's door. It opened — who the fuck didn't lock up in this day and age? — and she leant in to pop the boot. Closing the door quietly, she stuffed her doused torch in her pocket, moved to the back of the car, and raised the lid.

A shovel. A bag of unopened salt — the same brand as the empty bags at this morning's scene.

"Bugger me . . ." she breathed.

Boot lid down but left ajar, she strode to the front of the house and down the drive. Mike stood on the pavement, staring along the road. She told him what was in the boot.

"And I'm sure there's blood on the passenger seat. As far as you're concerned, I didn't look in it, right?" She raised her eyebrows.

"Of course you didn't. We'll just so happen to have a gander and find those things when we're actually allowed to," he said. "But bloody hell . . ."

"I know. If she doesn't answer, I want to burst in there, but things are still so flimsy, despite the clues, and Kribbs will have a pigging fit if we go in based on the shovel and salt I'm not even meant to have seen yet."

"Hmm. We'll have to play it by ear when we finally speak to her."

A patrol car arrived. Tammy Hill and Nicola Eccles got out, and Bethany explained the situation.

Then she said, "So we need you with us when we speak to her because she's odd. I thought she was ill and high on flu meds or something when we last saw her, but it might be a mental issue, and if she feels threatened, she may try something. Or she could have a meltdown. Either way, I'm more comfortable with the four of us present now I've got the jitters about this." Bethany scowled. "It's just a case of getting her to open the door — if she's even in." The idea of Miss Paling being out there scouting for another victim churned her stomach.

Once again at the door, Bethany knocked, surprised at it opening a minute or so later, Leeanne Paling standing there, sans the black shadows around her eyes, her lips a normal colour, her skin peach not white. Her hair had been brushed, and it shone, as though whatever ailment she'd suffered with had taken the brittleness with it when it had buggered off out of her system.

If she'd even been ill. She could have been high on drugs.

On the drugs found in Karl's blood? Is she on antidepressants and anxiety meds?

"Hello again, Leeanne, we need to ask you a few questions." Bethany managed to keep her tone even.

"Oh. Come in." She didn't sound the same. She was brighter, happier, as if a great weight had been lifted, although she was in pyjamas and a dressing gown — not a surprise, considering the time. "I've just woken up."

Bethany went in first, Mike behind her, Tammy and Nicola bringing up the rear. Bethany glanced at the scarf, making sure she hadn't imagined seeing it the first time, then across the hall at a pair of fluffy slippers upside down on the rad. She followed Leeanne into a living room, in darkness apart from the meagre light coming in through the window and those twinkling on the tree. Bethany reached out and flicked the wall switch, and the ceiling bulb lit up inside an old-fashioned, amber-coloured glass shade that needed taking down and dusting. It had to have been up there for decades.

Leeanne stood beside the tree next to the window. Hands clasped in front of her. Feet close together. Not appearing as a threat. Bethany smiled at her and moved aside to let Mike and the uniforms in.

"Would you like a drink?" Leeanne asked. "Tea? A little nip of something in it?" She giggled. "I'd have to make new nips, but I don't mind." She had a strange glint in her eye, but it vanished quickly.

"Um, we don't do 'nips' while on duty. And don't trouble yourself. Mike can make them." Bethany smiled again. Slanted her gaze at him: *Gives you a chance to nose around in the kitchen.*

"Oh, okay." Leeanne twirled her thumbs around each other. "But nips are good. They relax you."

The drugs Presley mentioned . . .

Leeanne cocked her head. "What did you want to ask me?"

Bethany reeled off the nights the murders had been committed. "Where were you?"

"In bed."

"You have no one to corroborate that?"

"No." She paused. "I think I slept in the caravan on one of those dates. I can't remember."

"Why would you sleep out there?"

"I like it."

"Why is there a candle on in the window?"

"For Maggie. So she can see me from Heaven."

Oh God, that's so sad. "Okay . . . Did you buy bags of salt recently?"

"Pardon?"

"Whose is that scarf in the hallway?"

"W-what?"

Someone retched behind Bethany, then coughed. Then came a quiet, "Oh my God . . ."

Bethany turned side-on, keeping Leeanne in her peripheral but looked at Tammy, then Nicola, who pointed ahead. Bethany faced that way again, staring at the tree. She frowned. *What am I meant to be seeing?*

"It's the end," Leeanne said. "That's what the problem is. The end. I thought that would be it, that I'd be happy, but you're here."

"Excuse me?" Bethany darted her gaze at the woman.

"This," Leeanne said, grabbing a candy cane and thrusting it towards her.

Tammy stepped forward, ready to intervene, cuffs in hand.

Bethany stared at the cane.

The end of a penis stared back at her.

CHAPTER TWENTY-TWO

"I've never called anyone else Candy Girl," he said, then grunted, his weight heavy on her.

The rocking. The pressure. She couldn't stand it.

Leeanne searched her mind for the stout farmer.

Please help me. Come and save me.

"Got your name on my neck," he went on. "So you'll know how special you are."

The farmer slung feed on the ground, and the yellow chicks and their russet-feathered mothers came running. Pecking, clucking.

She wished she was a chick.

"You're my chick," he said.

And she wished she wasn't one now.

A truck trundled up to the farmhouse, and a lady and her two children got out. The baker mother stepped outside, a tray of blueberry muffins held aloft. The kids squealed. Leeanne wanted to be the girl, and the boy would be her brother.

"You're mine," Dillon said. "Always mine."

Stout Farmer came over and ruffled Leeanne's hair. "Off you go and collect the eggs while the hens aren't looking."

She ran off, to the coops, working quickly so she didn't get an angry peck on her hand if a hen returned. Sixteen eggs, she had, and

Baker Mother could use them for more muffins. Maybe Leeanne would get one later along with her fizzy pop.

"Pretend you like it, for God's sake," Dillon said, his movements angry.

Leeanne ran with the egg basket to Stout Farmer, who took it and pulled her close to his side, shielding her, keeping her safe until it was time to go back to her real home, her bed, Dillon gone.

When it was okay to open her eyes, she found herself alone, shivering, the scent of Dillon's breath lingering.

Would it always be like this?

Would she ever have a night without Dillon?

* * *

Leeanne opened her eyes and was greeted with an unfamiliar ceiling. A strip light. Grey walls. A thin mattress beneath her. A blanket on top. Not the patchwork quilt.

Where was Mr Teddy?

She was really here, in the place she didn't want to be, another form of prison. She'd switched one for the other, except at least here, in the holding cell, she didn't have the familiar things from home triggering memories.

She'd thought, back when she'd put the *thing* on the candy cane blade, that it was over and she could live the life she'd always wanted. Sell the nunnery. Buy that farm. Be the baker mother and marry a stout farmer. Have a little girl of her own, giving her the dream life she'd never had. The best life.

This was the end. This was the terminus to her journey. Arrested. Waiting to speak to that policewoman, who'd said she'd be interviewed soon.

Should Leeanne tell her everything? If she talked about it, maybe her memories would no longer play out in her head, tormenting her. She'd been a fool to think it was over, that they wouldn't come back, but there she'd been, in her sleep, with Dillon there.

He'd always be there.

She closed her eyes, and once again, she'd have to rely on her other life to see her through. She brought in Stout

Farmer, who held his arms wide for her to run into them. Baker Mother appeared next to him, and they stood in the farmyard, the chicks twittering, the hens squawking, the lambs bleating.

She was home, a place inside her head, where she'd live out the rest of her days.

It was better than the real world.

Yes, she'd stay here.

Where she was safe.

CHAPTER TWENTY-THREE

Bethany sat opposite Leeanne, while Mike faced her solicitor, Lesley Fox. The tape was running, the video was on, and Tammy stood beside the closed door. The air had a 'breath held' feel about it, layered with expectancy, of wondering what was going to happen in this interview. Would it be a waste of time, Leeanne clamping up, or would they get what they wanted?

"Leeanne, I'd like to start by asking you again where you were on the following nights/early hours of the morning." Bethany listed the dates, sickened by the amount of them and all those lives lost because Leeanne had seen fit to end them. Despite the woman not having yet confessed and them only having circumstantial evidence, they would hopefully connect to conclusions of facts, because it had to be her.

"My client has already told you her answer when you asked her this at her home," Fox said, poking a finger at her papers on the table.

Bee in her bonnet or what? "I'm well aware of that, Miss Fox, but as you well know, I need it for the tape, and you preventing me from gathering the information I need isn't going to help your client, is it? While your client was in possession of a candy cane with the end of a penis on it, a striped scarf and a black Vectra, all of which link her to recent murders. We have a duty to find out why she has them and what she was doing on the nights and mornings in question."

Bethany shook her head slightly. While she understood Fox had a job to do, and the woman had to play it as she saw fit, if she was going to be annoying at every turn, Bethany would find it difficult to hide her rising temper. Bethany also had a bloody job to do, and that was getting this woman here to confess. "Leeanne?"

"I wasn't in bed." She tilted her head, as though listening. "Stout Farmer said to tell the truth." Leeanne kept her head bent.

"Stout Farmer? Who is that?" *Fuck me, is someone else in on this?*

"Mother Baker agrees. She'll give you a muffin if you behave yourself." Leeanne pulled at a loose thread on her grey sweatshirt cuff, one given to her here after they'd brought her in, and her nightwear had been taken as evidence.

"Who are these people?" Bethany asked.

"My mum and dad."

Bethany frowned. "We have it down that your father is unknown, and your mother, Zoe Paling, is deceased. Liver failure."

Leeanne laughed. "Liver failure . . . So funny."

"Why is that funny?"

"Because it is. She's my other mother. The nasty mother. She put me in a carrier bag." Leeanne tugged the thread off. It was long, like a stray hair. "She took me to Maggie, and Maggie let Dillon in."

"Dillon Orton?"

"He gave me a candy cane and a sausage."

Bethany gathered her thoughts. The candy cane was clearly significant — to Leeanne *and* to Dillon: the Candy Girl tattoo, the cane on the tree. When they'd had a good look at it earlier, they'd seen it wasn't an actual sweet but fashioned from metal and painted. A sharp blade had been put on the end, which was what the penis tip had been anchored to.

Who'd made it? Him or her?

But the sausage? No idea.

"Where did you get the candy cane from — the one that was at your house?" Bethany asked.

"I made it."

"Why is it important to you?"

"It's the beginning and the end."

"I don't understand. Would you elaborate?"

"I don't need to. It's easy. The beginning. The end."

Bethany resisted sighing. "While that may be simple to you, it isn't to me. I need more of an explanation."

"They stabbed themselves with it." Leeanne wrapped the thread around her finger. It was so tight, the skin whitened, her fingertip going red.

"You'll hurt yourself. Please remove that cotton." Anger bubbled, and Bethany took a deep breath to stop it coming out of her mouth in the form of words she might regret.

Leeanne unravelled it and let it fall to the table.

"Who stabbed themselves?" *The supposed suicides.* She'd been right that it hadn't been their choice.

"The first two Dillons."

"The first two weren't called Dillon. You know that. You left us notes telling us who they were."

"They were Dillon in my head."

"But you were also aware they weren't him — you had to have been if you took the time to write their names down and leave them at the scenes."

"A small part of me knew, when I was her, when I was *that* side, with my Maggie face."

Maggie face? "What's your Maggie face?"

"The one she had when she died."

"Why did you have a Maggie face? Was that *makeup* you had on when we first met you?"

Leeanne nodded. "If I was Maggie, in her clothes, I could bring the Dillons home, like she did. They'd trust me, like I trusted her, but she lied. Three times."

That explains the habit. "Were you there when she died?"

Leeanne bobbed her head. "I watched. Dillon and Zoe did it."

Interesting that she called her Zoe. "You mean your mother."

"No, Zoe. Baker Mother is my mum."

"You told me they're your parents. Where are they? We'll need to contact them to tell them you're here." Were these people aware she wasn't right in the head?

"They're at the farm."

"Which farm?"

"Best Life Farm."

Bethany glanced at Mike: *Have you heard of that?*

He shook his head. "Where is Best Life Farm?" He sounded patient, gentle.

"Up there," Leeanne said.

"Up where?" he asked.

"Up *there.*" Leeanne lifted her hands, pointed to her temples, and moved them back and forth.

It reminded Bethany of when she'd raised her hands before, then lowered them. "Why are you doing that?"

"Doing what?"

"That thing with your hands."

"It brings them here. Stout and Baker."

"I think we'd be better off bringing them here via a phone call, wouldn't you?" *Is she messing us about, or is this behaviour for real?*

"Nooooo," Leeanne said. "It brings them *here.*" She raised her eyes to indicate the top of her head.

"In your mind?" *Christ.*

Leeanne nodded, still twisting her hands. "They're here now."

Bethany added the proverbial two and two. "Okay, so they're something you made up, yes?"

"They looked after me when Dillon . . . did the things."

"The striped scarf. Is that yours?"

"No. Dillon didn't want it. Maggie bought it for him. We kept it. There's a hat and gloves, too. He's ungrateful. I got a Barbie. And her house. Not a Ken, though. Barbie didn't need a Ken, even though Dillon said she did. It's Christmas's fault. Maggie's. All of it."

"What did Christmas and Maggie do?"

"Shut up. I don't want to talk about that."

"Okay, let's move on. What about the drugs you used." *If she admits to that, we've at least got her on something concrete.*

"Maggie's and Zoe's meds. All mixed together. A magic potion."

"Why did you use it?"

"To put the Dillons to sleep." She stopped moving her hands and lowered them to the table. "I pushed him out of the window, you know. He kept climbing in."

"When did you do that?"

"I was little. Maggie said he wouldn't come back after that, but he did. Then Maggie was dead, and he moved in. Zoe drank gin all the time, and she fell asleep, and then he came to my room. Stout says what Dillon did was bad. Baker says Zoe was bad. But they don't say I'm bad. It wasn't my fault."

"The murders were your fault, though."

"*She* made me do it. Leeanne did it. My happy side wouldn't do anything like that."

"Who is your happy side?"

"Felicity Gray."

"Where does that name come from? Why did you choose that?"

"Stout gave it to me."

"I see." She didn't, but what she *had* gleaned was Leeanne Paling wasn't fit to be interviewed any longer, so there was just one question left to ask.

"Leeanne Paling, did you kill Karl Hartley, Caleb Pirtle, John Hancock and Dillon Orton?"

"Yes, she did. But I didn't have anything to do with it. Felicity Gray didn't do it."

"Okay, Leeanne Paling, I am arresting you for the murders of Karl Hartley, Caleb Pirtle, John Hancock and Dillon Orton. You do not have to say anything, but it may harm your defence if you do not mention when questioned something which you later rely on in court. Anything you do say may be given in evidence."

"Leeanne's a naughty girl. She's Candy Girl." She lifted her head and stared at Bethany. "Felicity is a good girl. Can I go home to the farm now? I want my best life."

Bethany diverted her gaze to the solicitor.

Lesley Fox's eyes misted. "No, Leeanne, you have to remain here for the time being." She looked at Bethany. "I want my client to be ass—"

"Yes, we'll discuss that in private." Bethany gave the spiel to end the interview, then stood.

Tammy walked round to assist Leeanne, holding her upper arm while she escorted her, cuffed, from the room. The door closed after them, and Bethany let out a ragged sigh.

"That woman isn't well," she said.

"Like I was going to say before you interrupted, I want my client assessed." Fox gathered her papers and stuffed them in her briefcase.

"We'll get to that now." Bethany rubbed her forehead. "God knows what she's been through."

Fox relaxed her shoulders. "Oh, I thought I was going to have to fight you all the way. Some officers don't play it by the book . . ."

"You've heard what they say about 'assume', haven't you?"

Fox's cheeks reddened. "I'm sorry. If you knew how many times I've had to push for interviews to be stopped in a situation like Leeanne's, only to be ignored because the officers just want details."

"I'm not other officers. Mike isn't other officers. When it's clear someone has mental issues and is hurting — yes, she's hurting — they need all the help on offer, not a copper badgering them. She's confused, she thinks she's two people. She has the idea she has more parents, who live in her head. She doesn't need me pushing for information. And for the record, myself and Mike are possibly rare in that we do have empathy for killers. People like Leeanne . . . She's been through something terrible to have killed the way she did. While I don't agree with how she dealt with it, sometimes people snap. She's broken, her thought processes are broken, and she did what she thought was the right thing."

Fox nodded. "In that case, nice to meet you, Bethany Smith." She shoved her hand out.

Bethany shook it. "Nice to meet you, too. Now, go and do your best for her. She has no one left to fight her corner."

With that, her eyes stinging —*for Pete's sake!*— Bethany exited the room, sad for the dead — *but not Dillon, I won't be sad for him* — and sad for the woman whose mind was so twisted by what had happened to her that she possibly lived half her life in reality, half out of it.

She walked to the car park, her day far from over, Mike at her heels. In the car, belted up, she drove towards the nunnery. Isabelle and one of her teams were there, and Bethany wanted to walk around to get a feel for the place — also to see if there was any more evidence. The Vectra had been taken away, as had the scarf, the candy cane and that ghastly thing on the end of it. Just before she'd interviewed Leeanne, Isabelle had sent word that they'd found a basement, and it needed to be seen to be believed.

"I'm not sure I want to know what happened to her," she said to Mike. "Although it's obvious what Dillon did to her. The sausage."

"Absolutely revolting. I'm glad he's dead."

"Do you think she's been looking for him ever since he moved to York?" She turned into Leeanne's street.

"No. There were years between him leaving and the first murder. Maybe she was happy for a time. Her mother died, perhaps she felt free then. Something must have set her off."

"I wonder what it was?"

"I'd say him returning to Shadwell, but we know he caught a train here after the first three murders, so it can't be that."

"Candy canes are brought out at Christmas. She said it was Christmas's fault."

"Maybe that's it then. Whatever that cane means, if she saw one, it could have triggered her."

Bethany parked behind the SOCO van — seemed that was the story of her life lately.

Togged up, log signed, a quick hello to Glen Underby at the front door, and they stepped inside. Officers in white suits did their jobs, and a SOCO nodded at Bethany and pointed to a door in the kitchen.

"Isabelle's waiting for you," he said.

She opened it and led the way down, going through another doorway at the bottom.

Oh.

What. The. Fuck?

Drawings filled the walls, awful pictures of death, blood, savagery. Devil's with horns. A pole was bolted to the floor and ceiling, a metal one sticking out of it, while a shorter, wooden one stood to the side.

Isabelle turned from bending over at the far end where she'd been peering at something. "Ah, hello." She smiled. "I've finally found the button."

"The button?" Bethany frowned and moved closer, skirting a SOCO on his knees.

"There's a speaker up there, look." Isabelle pointed to a corner. "And upstairs, in Leeanne's bedroom, there's a computer, no password needed, and when we jiggled the mouse, it showed a recording app and a camera in this room, although we haven't found that yet. There were some files of her chanting stuff: *Kill yourself, you will bleed out, you will die.* Nice." She shrugged. "The button is what must turn it on. And that big pole there . . . They were tied to it — that's my guess anyway. There's a belt, a padlock on it."

Bethany turned to see.

Mike pointed. "What the hell's that hole in the floor over there?"

"We've shone a torch into it. A pipe. One of my boys has put a probe down there, drawn some water. The inside of the pipe has dried blood on the lip. Who knows, with that hose beside it, maybe she cleaned the place and the water went that way."

"Who would want an open pipe in their house?" Mike shook his head.

"You can tell it's mega years old," Isabelle said. "Probably something they did in the olden days. If not, who knows why it's there. Might make for interesting Googling in your spare time. Did you get to speak to her yet? Going by these pictures, she's one messed-up woman."

"She is. We had to abandon it. She needs a mental health assessment."

"Thought that would be the case when you told me about the dick on the cane spike. That's not usual behaviour, is it."

Mike sighed. "That was difficult to see."

"Make you want to protect your privates, did it?" Isabelle laughed. "Oh my days, did you see Presley go to do that at the last scene?"

"Aww, don't be mean," Bethany said. "It even had me twitching, and I don't own any dangly bits."

"Oh, before I forget . . ." Isabelle used her inner wrist to rub her cheek. "Out in the back garden, there's a large metal drum. Rusty old thing. Something's been burnt in it recently."

"Did a search of the house find the habit?" Bethany prayed it had.

"Nope, so my guess is she set fire to all the things that would incriminate her, although why she kept that piece of dick . . ."

"I don't understand that either." Mike cleared his throat.

"We also found that missing toenail. The place has been bleached," Isabelle went on, "so she knew what she was doing."

"Was she Leeanne or Felicity, though, that's the question," Bethany said.

"Who the hell is Felicity?" Isabelle asked.

"Long story." Bethany blinked away the burn of tears. "A pretty sad one from what we can gather by putting all the pieces together."

"I don't want to know." Isabelle held her gloved hand up. "Hey, guess what?"

"What . . ." Bethany waited for more obscene evidence to be brought to her attention.

"We all get to enjoy Christmas."

Hmm, there was that, but would it be enjoyable? By herself? Really?

"About that," she said, turning to Mike. "I think I will go with you to your mum's after all. What shall I bring with me? Chocolates? Some sherry?"

"Anything but candy canes." He grimaced.

They laughed, all three of them, in a place where men had been drugged and told to stab themselves. Where, as Presley had informed her earlier, they'd eaten raw meat, and she *really* didn't want to know why that was. Not when Christmas was calling, a few days off where she could recharge and spend time with her best friend, Mike. The other one, Vin, well, his whisper floated inside her head, and she smiled, tears stinging.

"Have a good one, Beth. Love you . . ."

THE END

THE JOFFE BOOKS STORY

We began in 2014 when Jasper agreed to publish his mum's much-rejected romance novel and it became a bestseller.

Since then we've grown into the largest independent publisher in the UK. We're extremely proud to publish some of the very best writers in the world, including Joy Ellis, Faith Martin, Caro Ramsay, Helen Forrester, Simon Brett and Robert Goddard. Everyone at Joffe Books loves reading and we never forget that it all begins with the magic of an author telling a story.

We are proud to publish talented first-time authors, as well as established writers whose books we love introducing to a new generation of readers.

We have been shortlisted for Independent Publisher of the Year at the British Book Awards three times, in 2020, 2021 and 2022, and for the Diversity and Inclusivity Award at the Independent Publishing Awards in 2022.

We built this company with your help, and we love to hear from you, so please email us about absolutely anything bookish at: feedback@joffebooks.com.

If you want to receive free books every Friday and hear about all our new releases, join our mailing list: www.joffebooks.com/contact

And when you tell your friends about us, just remember: it's pronounced Joffe as in coffee or toffee!

ALSO BY EMMY ELLIS

DI BETHANY SMITH

Book 1: THE COLD CALL KILLER
Book 2: THE CREEPY-CRAWLY KILLER
Book 3: THE SCREWDRIVER KILLER
Book 4: THE SCORCHED SKIN KILLER
Book 5: THE STREET PARTY KILLER
Book 6: THE CANDY CANE KILLER

DETECTIVE CAROL WREN MYSTERIES

Book 1: SPITE YOUR FACE
Book 2: HOLD YOUR BREATH
Book 3: GUILT BURNS HOLES
Book 4: BEST SERVED COLD
Book 5: BLOOD RUNS DEEP

Printed in Dunstable, United Kingdom

64598796R00109